Grimworld

Grimworld

Avery Moray

OUR STREET
BOOKS

Winchester, UK
Washington, USA

JOHN HUNT PUBLISHING

First published by Our Street Books, 2018
Our Street Books is an imprint of John Hunt Publishing Ltd., Laurel House, Station Approach,
Alresford, Hants, SO24 9JH, UK
office@jhpbooks.com
www.johnhuntpublishing.com
www.ourstreet-books.com

For distributor details and how to order please visit the 'Ordering' section on our website.

Text copyright: Avery Moray 2017

ISBN: 978 1 78904 157 6
978 1 78904 158 3 (ebook)
Library of Congress Control Number: 2018946915

A CIP catalogue record for this book is available from the British Library.

Design: Stuart Davies

UK: Printed and bound by CPI Group (UK) Ltd, Croydon, CR0 4YY
US: Printed and bound by Thomson-Shore, 7300 West Joy Road, Dexter, MI 48130

We operate a distinctive and ethical publishing philosophy in
all areas of our business, from our global network of authors to
production and worldwide distribution.

Contents

To my parents for their support
Mark for all of his help
And Alan for making this possible

"All that really belongs to us is time; even he who has nothing else has that."
Baltasar Gracián

Chapter 1

Henry Bats Acquires a Pocket Watch

The Grimworld was particularly dark today. Henry Bats, a boy of thirteen and shorter than most, left his school for the narrow, foggy streets of the Penumbra Region. He looked up and saw black through the many buildings piled together like a wonky wedding cake. The only light came from the purple and green streetlamps that shone onto his pale face.

Out of the corner of his eye, he spotted a Gloom Ghast trailing behind him, its fuzzy gray outline popping in and out of focus on the sidewalk. If he looked at it too quickly, it would disappear. But Henry liked the Ghasts, so he only snuck glimpses.

He arrived at Frank's Peculiar Pets, a shop signified by a flashing snake cartoon. Inside, he found Frank behind the counter with a rat on his shoulder. A chorus of chirps, squawks, and squeaks filled the store from its snake-tiled floor to the vine-covered ceiling. The hefty, bald owner looked up from his paperwork. "Henry, here to help with the frogs?"

"Nah, just need some crickets. How's Tuna?"

"Won't quit nibbling my ear." Frank scratched the rat's head and left his papers for a glass case. His scarred fingers reached inside to pluck crickets into a plastic container. "Buggers always give me a hard time," he mumbled.

Henry shuffled to each tank, peering inside at the salamanders, spiders, rats, and frogs. He himself had a yellow fang-toothed tarantula named Corn Chip.

"What's this orange spider?" he said, peering through the glass at long, thin legs connected to a round body.

"Called a Pillowcase Spider cause that's where they like to lay eggs." Frank handed him the cricket container. "But what's really interesting is the Double-Headed Snapwinder."

He showed Henry to a black snake with two heads. Its four eyes watched them, tongues flicking.

"Cool, where'd you get it?"

"Dealer from the Purple Market. Now, tell the crazy lady I could use some worms."

"Come on, Frank, she yells at me every time."

"You know how hard worms are to come by. Now scoot."

"Alright." He sighed.

Henry navigated through Grimworld's many side streets and alleyways towards home, the Gloom Ghast never far behind. He entered a residential area, each porch glowing with ectolanterns to ward off entities. He stopped when he came to an old house squeezed between two crooked apartment complexes. The worm lady sat on the porch in her rocking chair, a brown box on her lap. She wore a bathrobe, her crusty eyes lit up with her yellow lantern. Small worms poked out from her frizzy hair and dove back in. The kids in Henry's school dared each other to peek through her windows, and many reported seeing hundreds of worms wriggling on the carpet.

He walked to the porch but didn't go up the steps. Something about the squirmy, eyeless bodies gave him the creeps.

"Frank asked for worms again," he said.

The lady's wrinkles scrunched up into a scowl. "You tell that bald-headed brute he'll never touch my babies. He'd feed them to those wretched, horrible creatures. Be gone, boy, and your pet Ghast too."

She jerked her head to the shy Gloom Ghast and it disappeared. Her box jiggled slightly and she looked down, poked her finger in, and whispered to the contents inside.

"I tried," Henry muttered, and crossed the street. The Bats' residence was in an apartment alley below a Botsworth Tram track that ran over the roof and shook the whole building. His family's door had an orange ectolantern hung out on the front.

Inside was the kitchen, complete with black and white tiles and sickly green walls, the counter messy with food splatters and unwashed dishes. His twelve-year-old sister, Hattie, was seated at the table reading. She wore her usual long-sleeved, black dress with a bow on the back of her blonde head.

"Hello, Henry." She hummed in an off-key choir song.

"You've been humming that for days, stop already." He slung his backpack onto the table.

"But the Nightspook likes it."

"Tell it to go away."

"I like the company."

Henry rolled his eyes and went to his room. It was covered in comic book posters. Grave Stalker, Lady Haggish, The Steel Chancellor, and his favorite, the one and only Captain Grim. Comic books organized by title lined his bookshelf and action figures cluttered his desk.

He opened the lid to Corn Chip's enclosure, dumped a cricket inside, and stood still, listening by a Grave Stalker poster. From the other side of the wall, which was Hattie's bedroom, came three knocks. The hair on Henry's arms stood on end and he stepped back.

"Definitely a Nightspook," he told Corn Chip, who was already in the midst of a crunchy dinner.

Nightspooks were a pesky spirit entity that latched onto people or buildings until they were banished. One had once chosen to reside in the Bats' bathroom and enjoyed putting Henry's toothbrush in the toilet.

He heard the front door open and close, followed by his father's loud footsteps. Back in the kitchen, he found Gobbert Bats sitting across from Hattie, his expansive stomach pushed out to the table. He shared Henry's brown, unruly hair and gray eyes.

"Have a seat, Hen," he said, patting the chair next to him.

Henry plopped down.

3

"The both of you close your eyes and hold out your hand. Now...open."

Henry felt a sticky blob in his palm and looked down to find a gummy candy. It was gray and covered with green slime.

Hattie smiled. "Are these the new brains?"

"That they are, little miss."

Gobbert worked for Gelatin Skeleton Candy Company. The front door opened again and Henry's mom arrived with an armful of groceries. She walked with light steps and had blonde hair like Hattie.

"I'll help you, Mildred," Gobbert said.

She peeked over the paper bags. "Hi kids."

"Hi, Mom."

His parents bustled around the kitchen preparing a basket of soggy chips and a glazed meatloaf with black, bubbling goo, while Henry and Hattie did their homework at the table. His sister rapidly filled out her math sheet, Henry plodding away at his.

"Hey, I'll give you my brain if you finish this for me," he whispered.

"No way, do your own."

"Dinner's ready," Mildred announced. "Hen, get your grandfather."

"It's Hattie's turn," he said, staring his sister down.

"Is not."

"I got him yesterday."

"Did not."

Mildred shielded herself with an oven mitt from the mildly explosive goo. "Just go, Henry."

Glaring at Hattie, he stomped up to the attic, occupied by Flemm Bats, and knocked on the door. When there came no reply, he creaked it open. "Grandpa?"

A puff of pipe smoke blew in Henry's face and a somber classical tune from a phonograph reached his ears. Flemm was sitting in his chair, surrounded by a few lit candles and taxidermy books, as per usual. His long nose was stuck in the pages of Just like Couch Reupholstery.

He yanked out his pipe. "What do you want? I'm busy."

"Time for dinner, Grandpa," Henry said, airing out the smoke.

"Bah, waste of time."

"But we're having meatloaf."

He squinted at Henry and snapped the book shut. "Fine."

At the table they passed around the bubbling, oozing meatloaf, grandpa Flemm sulking in his chair.

"We learned about the Lightworld myth in class today," Hattie said through a bite of meatloaf. "The lamp in the sky."

"Quite a tale, don't you think?" Gobbert heaved a slice onto his plate as a Botsworth Tram passed overhead and rattled the dishes.

"But they have written records from when the light disappeared."

"Anyone can make those up."

"And you, Hen? What did you learn?" Mildred said.

"Boring stuff." Henry gripped his glass of Fungaid to keep it from falling over.

"You should really pay more attention in school, Henry. Gobbert, would you pass the salt?"

"Salt?" Flemm jumped in his chair. "Back in the war, I remember sweat – *salty* sweat, running down my face, all those long days and nights keeping watch."

The war had been a small protest against the mayor for raising the price of lettuce.

"That's nice, Dad," Mildred said.

"You don't appreciate the hardships we went through." He sat back in his chair with a deep frown.

After dinner, Hattie grabbed Henry by the wrist.

"What do you want, Hattie? I'm tired."

"I have something to show you." She dragged him to her very purple room and they stood before a shelf lined with her porcelain doll collection, each plagued by a crack or chip or missing body part.

"Fascinating," Henry said, ready to leave.

"Just watch, we've been practicing." She cleared her throat and declared, "Bertha." A doll in a faded red dress with missing hair raised its arm and waved at them.

"Ruby," Hattie said and a doll, with half her face gone, winked at them with her porcelain eyelid.

Henry lifted an eyebrow. "How are you doing that?"

"The Nighspook."

"You trained it?"

"It's not a dog, Henry. It just likes to play games."

"You need friends."

She folded her arms. "You're one to talk."

"I'm going to my room. Keep training your pet."

Henry entered his room and flopped down onto his bed, half-listening to the TV boom through the living room wall. He could make out the words 'Walpog infestation...Shadow Region... Teacups.' He reread Captain Grim comics and took out a sheet of paper. Pencil in hand, he sketched out his own superhero he had come up with; Shadow Man. It ended up looking like a squiggly mess and he scrapped it.

His parents said goodnight and Henry fell asleep in his Captain Grim sheets. He was dreaming about a giant meatloaf with legs when he awoke to a noise. He rolled over and tried to fall back asleep. A minute later he heard the noise again, a sort of thump. His eyes squinted at the alarm clock. 3 A.M.

"Hattie?" he yawned.

No reply. He pried his eyes open and lifted his head a few inches. As there were no windows in the room, the only light came from the glowing numbers on the alarm clock. But there across the room, darker than dark, was a shadow in the vague shape of a person. Henry blinked rapidly, hoping his mind was playing tricks on him, but the black mass remained. He sat up, heart pounding. There were no distinguishable features on the shadow, but he knew whatever it was, was watching him.

"Hello?" he whispered.

The mass seemed to shiver, and as if from nowhere, there came a voice. "Hello." It was deep and muted, as if underwater, but he heard it clearly. He made himself as still as possible.

"What are you?"

"A Nightspook."

"Nightspooks are invisible. And they can't talk."

"You're wrong."

The shadow crept closer. It glided across the floor until it was beside his nightstand. Henry repeated in his mind that Nightspooks were harmless.

"Hattie told me about you," it said.

Henry had trouble getting his words out. "Oh, she did?"

"I need your help."

"How about you ask Hattie? She can be really helpful, you know."

The edges of the figure became sharper. "No. You."

Henry slowly lay down and pulled the blanket over his face, speaking through the fabric. "I really have to get some sleep, so if you could just leave."

After a minute of silence, Henry poked his head out from the sheet. The shadow was still there, hovering above him, and it was growing larger. His palms were slick with sweat. "I guess you're not leaving."

"No." Its voice was louder.

"What do you need help with?"

"I need something."

"What do you need?"

"Come with me."

"I really don't have time right now."

The shadow expanded further. "Come. Now."

"I can't." Henry shrunk into his pillow.

The black stretched out, covering the bed, its voice vibrating in his ears. "Come now. There will be a reward."

Henry knew if he didn't go, the Nightspook wouldn't go away, or worse, it would attach itself to him. "What kind of reward?"

"Anything your heart desires."

He thought about what his heart desired. "A first edition of Captain Grim?"

"Yes. Come."

"What if I don't go?"

"No escape," the shadow boomed and completely engulfed the bed with its mass.

Henry gulped. "Promise you'll leave me alone after?"

"Yes."

He squeezed his fists and released. "Fine."

The mass shrunk and disappeared through the door. Henry got up, not bothering to change out of his pajamas. The roaring snore of Gobbert echoed throughout the house and he moved with every exhale, making sure to step over the squeaky floorboards. The shadow was waiting for him outside, now a suspended lump the size of his head.

"Follow me."

It darted down the alleyway and Henry ran to keep up, the cold air creeping down his spine. He glanced up at the sky, a dark pit of black. The night was still and empty besides a few lone cars that sped by and the rumble of a Botsworth Tram. They came to the beginning of a street called Sable Avenue, where a graveyard stretched all the way to the forest. The piece of land was enclosed by a spiked fence and dotted with spindly, lifeless trees. Small yellow ectolanterns lit up each grave.

Henry backed up. "I'm not going near the forest, no way."

"No. Follow me."

A fog swirled around Henry's feet and the shadow led him past the gate and puffed large in front of a marble crypt that took up its own section in the graveyard. The name Jacoby Dread was etched above the iron door, the crypts of many other Dreads nearby – Wilhelmina, Prudence, Ezekiel, Wilmer, Zachary.

The Nightspook said, "Go inside."

These were the words Henry least wanted to hear. He slowly put his hand on the cold crypt handle and pulled. The door opened with a screech to reveal a stone casket lit by a lantern in the corner. He stepped inside with wobbly legs. The Nightspook swooped in and hovered above the casket. "Open."

Henry shook his head and turned to leave. "Nope. No way."

The shadow spread out like a black waterfall and blocked the door. "Open," it repeated.

Left with no choice, Henry squeezed his eyes shut and held out his shaky hands.

"Captain Grim first edition," he whispered to himself.

He gripped the casket lid and struggled to lift the weight, pushing it up inch by inch. Finally, he was able to shove it far enough to fall and rest on the crypt wall. With one eye barely open he looked down, afraid of what he might find. But instead of a body, there was a pocket watch on top of another marble slab that covered what lay beneath. The watch was flat with a long gold chain and the image of a crow etched into the center.

"Turn to 12 o'clock," the shadow said.

Henry picked up the watch. It was cold and heavy in his hand. He pulled on the crown and twisted the hands clockwise until the time was 12 o'clock. The figure shivered and whatever it was made up of separated. Black wisps dissolved into the crypt ceiling.

"What about Captain Grim?" Henry called, and reached out to brush his hand through the remaining mist. It tangled around his fingers and disappeared like smoke. The light from the ectolantern went out. Henry was now alone in the dark crypt with strange, ghostly noises coming from the forest beyond. He tossed the watch back onto the slab and hurried out. The fog had thickened and wrapped around his pajama bottoms as he shut the door to Jacoby Dread's final resting place. Not wanting to see what made the forest noises, he ran home and collapsed onto his pillow, burrowing under the covers to get warm. The weight of exhaustion closed his eyes and he fell into a deep sleep. It seemed only minutes had passed when the alarm buzzed him awake.

"Already?" Henry fumbled for the off button. Images flashed through his mind. A walking meatloaf. Crows. Shadows. Graveyard. Pocket watch. His eyes flew open. "Ridiculous," he assured himself. "Nightspooks don't talk."

He heaved himself up and felt a thump on his chest. He looked down, and there, around his neck, was the gold chain with the pocket watch on the end.

Chapter 2

Madam Desmona Advises Against Truffles

Henry touched the pocket watch, sure he was imagining things or *something*, but it was just as firm and cold as any metal would be. Upon closer examination, he found that all the numbers had disappeared except for the 12 and the 2. The hour hand had also disappeared, the minute still pointing to the 12. He popped open the watch face and tried to move the minute hand, but it wouldn't budge. He grabbed the chain and tried to yank it over his head, but it was too small. He even tried breaking it, his heart sinking as he realized the watch wasn't coming off by force. This was the work of a Nightspook after all, although he had never heard of them attaching objects to people.

A knock on the door startled him.

"Hen, breakfast. Get your grandfather," Mildred called. He stuffed the watch under his pajama shirt and raced up the stairs, shouting to Flemm that breakfast was ready. He jumped into his chair at the table, inhaled a bowl of Sugar Slugs, and before anyone could sit down, he was dressed and ready to leave.

"Did you take your Steel Chancellor Vita-D pill?" Mildred asked, but he was already out the door.

Henry took a deep breath and inhaled the damp air. The streets were thick with fog, the sky barely tinged with light. He patted the watch underneath his shirt. "Some reward."

Hurrying, so he wouldn't be late for school, he tried to retrace his steps from the night before. After asking for directions, he was able to locate the graveyard at the beginning of Sable Street. It was time to do some investigating.

He crossed through the gate into the silent cemetery. Jacoby Dread's crypt stood tall and gloomy with gray, dull marble. The door screeched open of its own accord and Henry forced himself to step inside. The casket was closed, the ectolantern dimly lighting the interior.

He pushed the casket lid up and as expected, the top layer was empty. The crow pocket watch was indeed around his neck.

"Now for the hard part," he muttered to himself.

He placed his hands on the bottom marble section and took a deep breath. The slab lifted in his sweaty palms and he dared to look at what he uncovered.

"Nothing," he said, his shoulders relaxing.

There were no bones, no body, no objects. Just empty space. He closed the casket and ran back to the graveyard entrance, hurrying to Oozefant Middle School, a gray brick building surrounded by a chain link fence, which Henry thought quite resembled a prison. Blood red lamps lit up the front of the school, which featured a banner with the school's mascot on it; a mosquito.

He made it to Ms Squid's class just before the bell rang. The students discussed what they watched on TV the night before, or what their parents did to annoy them, or how cute Casper Tombly is in grade 8. All Henry could think about was standing in a graveyard at three in the morning with a Nightspook. The watch around his neck was another issue. How was he going to get it off?

Lunch came and he balanced a tray of gloopy, colorless food all the way to the library. He scanned the shelves and found a book on the entities of Grimworld. He sat on the floor, took a bite of gloop, and found the Nightspook entry on page 467. It read:

Nightspook (A.K.A. Night Knocker)
Appearance: Typically transparent
First discovery: Umbra Region
Occurrence: Common

Description: Invisible beings that attach themselves to buildings, objects, or people.

Signs of presence: Moved objects, knocking.

"Doesn't say anything about a watch." Henry sighed.

"Not in the comic book section today, Mr Bats?"

He looked up to find Mr McPlume, the librarian, hovering above him. He had a narrow nose, gray bushy hair, and tended to wear vests with bowties.

"Nah, just doing some studying."

"I have a new issue of Corpse Boy, want me to pull it for you?"

He shoved the entity book back onto the shelf. "No, I think I'm going to eat lunch in the cafeteria today."

"That's unlike you," Mr McPlume said and went off to shush a group of girls.

Henry ate lunch at a table where everyone quietly did their homework and halfheartedly worked on his. After school, he drifted down the hall, lost in thought. Classmates passed by, gathering their belongings at their lockers. Henry absentmindedly looked up, not paying attention to anything in particular, and noticed a tall, dark-skinned boy leaving a classroom. He was hunched over with his hands shoved in his pockets, his brown eyes serious. Henry had seen him before, but today there was something that caught his attention. He stopped in his tracks, transfixed. Around the boy's neck was what appeared to be a pocket watch. After a moment of hesitation, Henry bounded outside and followed the boy through the gloomy streets. He spoke up when they had gone a few blocks.

"Hey," he called.

The boy kept walking.

"Is that a pocket watch?"

The boy stopped in front of a mish-mash of squished houses and turned around. Henry caught up and saw that the watch, silver instead of gold, had a wolf etched in the center.

"My name is Henry Bats. Last night, well a Nightspook asked for help and I ended up with this." He pulled out the watch from his shirt. "I can't get it off."

The boy stared at him.

"Did the same thing happen to you?"

"That wasn't a Nightspook," the boy said and narrowed his eyes.

"It wasn't?"

"It's called a Vytiper. Do you have any idea what you just did?"

Henry slowly shook his head. "No."

The boy spat, "Look, I'm not going to help you just because we fell for the same trick," and began to walk away.

"Wait, what do you mean by trick?"

"You're on your own."

"But I don't know what I did wrong."

The boy whirled around and marched back, eyes locked with Henry's. "You gave away part of your life, that's what you did."

"My life?"

"Your lifespan. Let's say you were supposed to die at 60, you might die at 40 now. Got it?"

Henry stumbled backwards. "That's impossible."

"Don't believe me? Moulde Library, Mutter's Grand List of Entities, page 708. By the way," he leaned forward and grabbed Henry's watch, inspecting it, "looks like you'll die in 10 years."

With that, the boy left, leaving Henry with his mouth open, staring into the distance. A Botsworth Tram made its way through the housing mess and rumbled him out of his stupor. His body felt light as he floated by Frank's Peculiar Pets, past the worm lady, and past his house. Barely aware of how he got there, he found himself in the Moulde Library guidebook section with the latest edition of Mutter's Grand List of Entities in hand. Mrs Mutter's entry on the Vytiper was as follows:

Vytiper: Information minimal. The Vytiper is newly discovered with rare occurrence. The form is a black mass that possesses the ability to speak. I have only acquired two case studies and have determined encounters conclude with a random amount of lifespan taken by use of a pocket watch with the image of an animal. Each minute on the watch represents one year of remaining life, with the leftover number representing approximate death arrival. For example, if the number 7 is left, there are 35 years left to live. The minute hand acts as a countdown. No reversal has been found. More research needed.

Case Study #1: Fenella Shakes, age 14, and her mother came to me inquiring about a shadow mass that lured her to an unmarked grave. Her watch was gold with a cricket and the number 3 remaining. I worked to uncover the meaning of the watch until Fenella passed away 15 years later from unknown circumstances.

Case Study #2: Located Ralph Moon, age 9, who had a bronze watch with a cat and the number 1. He described a similar shadow figure to Fenella that led him to the grave of Elsphat de Gory. Ralph passed away 5 years later. I was then able to determine the meaning of the watches.

Henry snapped the book shut and sat on the floor, pulling his knees to his chest. His head spun. Of course, he knew he would die eventually, everyone would. But this was different. This meant he only had ten years left to live. His body fell back against the bookshelf and a knot formed in his stomach.

That night at dinner he sat sullen-faced while Hattie complained about the Nightspook vanishing. "I can't do the doll trick anymore," she whined.

"Well, that's just too bad." Henry stabbed his fork through a crusty bread pile.

"What's up with you?"

"Are you feeling alright, Hen?" Mildred reached over a bowl of bright orange soup and felt his forehead.

He looked around the table and opened his mouth, ready to tell everyone what had happened the night before, but stopped. Instead, he brushed Mildred's hand away and mumbled, "I'm fine." He didn't want to upset his family, not until he had things figured out.

The next day, as soon as the bell rang for school to be out, he packed up his stuff and hurried to the entrance to wait. It was slightly brighter than usual, the sky a solid pigeon gray. For once the Penumbra Region almost didn't need the lampposts that constantly buzzed throughout the city.

The boy with the pocket watch finally emerged and Henry fell into step beside him, matching his pace. The boy gave no acknowledgement and kept his gaze straight. They walked several blocks in silence until the boy halted. "I said I wasn't going to help you."

Henry squared his shoulders. "But there's got to be a way to get these things off. Don't you think we should work together?"

"No."

"Why not?"

"I'm figuring it out alone."

"But two brains are better than one, right?"

"I don't think so." The boy walked on.

"How much time do you have left?" Henry said, right beside him again. "Can you at least tell me your name?"

Silence.

Henry turned around. "Fine, be alone."

Had a strange pocket watch not been around his neck, he would have gone to Frank's to help manage the Fire Snoots. But today, he made his way to a bench beside a flickering lamppost in the cemetery on Sable Avenue. A thick white fog crept on the ground. By now, the sky had gone from gray to black.

Henry put his head in his hands, thoughts whizzing around

like flies. "What if I can't reverse it?" he muttered to himself. "Who would take care of Corn Chip?"

He watched the fog tendrils billow around his feet, some looping in and out of his shoelaces. Footsteps echoed through the graveyard and he snapped his head up. A figure loomed in the distance, too far away to distinguish who, or what, it was. When it came closer, Henry saw it was the boy with the wolf watch. He stopped at an intricately engraved tombstone, staring down with his hands in his pockets. After a few minutes, he turned around and jumped when he noticed Henry. They stared at each other. Finally, the boy came over and sat on the other end of the bench. He cleared his throat. "Langley Skullfield. Call me Lang."

Henry reached his hand across the bench and Lang briefly shook it. "Henry Bats."

"I know, you told me. About earlier, I'm sorry I wouldn't talk to you." Lang kicked the tip of his shoe into the dirt.

Henry shrugged. "It's alright."

"I knew someone else who got tricked. I didn't figure out what the watches meant until it was too late for him."

Henry stared at a particularly lively fog tendril. "Sorry. When did it happen to you?"

"I was nine. That grave, Greta Flingbossom," he pointed to the tombstone he visited, "is where the Vytiper made me stand."

"I was over there, at Jacoby Dread's crypt."

They both sat for a while, listening to a bloated toad croak. Henry leaned forward and stole a glance at Lang's watch. The only numbers that remained were the 12 and 1.

"Lang?"

"Yes?"

"When are you supposed to die?"

He responded plainly, "Soon. The minute hand is almost at the one, so I'd guess a couple of weeks."

Henry shot up from the bench. "Then what are we doing

sitting here?"

"It's fine. I've had a lot of time to get used to the idea."

"We should at least go to the police or something."

"Already been. But you know they don't deal with entities."

Henry shook his head. "Unbelievable. Have you tried getting it off?"

"Not for a while."

"Is it even possible?"

Lang shrugged and Henry pulled him up from the bench. "Come on."

"Where are we going?"

"I don't know, but we have to do something."

They struck off through Grimworld without a particular destination in mind.

"Have you tried changing the watch time?"

Lang nodded. "Yep."

"What about seeing an entity removal expert?"

"I saved enough money to pay for one. They had no idea what a Vytiper was and tried to figure it out. No luck."

"Mrs Mutter knew what it was."

"She died a few years ago."

"Oh."

They ended up at a shopping street clustered with lit signs, most advertising antiques and knick-knacks. Henry noticed a glowing purple one that read: Madam Desmona – Fortunes Told for a Bit of Gold. He scratched his head. "Have you tried a psychic?"

"I don't think that would do much good."

"But why not? It's worth a try."

Lang reluctantly followed Henry into the little building. The reception room was decorated with purple wood panels and colorful lamps that emanated dim light. They inhaled a heavy, throat-clogging perfume. Henry scrunched up his nose.

Sobs and nose blowing came from behind a door. It burst open and an elderly man stepped out with a handful of tissues. He looked at the boys, sobbed a tearful, "Walpogs," and departed. Lang glanced at Henry with raised eyebrows. A deep, scratchy voice commanded, "Enter."

The room they went in was draped with black curtains and candles. Glass orbs gently swayed back and forth from the ceiling and a crow, who was perched on a crystal branch, bobbed her head and cawed as the boys stepped inside. Henry shuddered when he saw Madam Desmona. She was sat at a round table wearing a deep red, velvety dress that engulfed her round figure. A spider web tattoo covered the side of her face framed by white, wild hair. A variety of stones, cards, and figurines were laid out on the table before her.

"Sit." She waved a veiny hand in front of her. "Now, what brings you handsome boys to Madam Desmona?" Her lips curled into a smile, pale eyes glinting in the candlelight.

Henry spoke first. "I don't have a lot of money, but we were hoping you could help us. Have you ever heard of a Vytiper?"

"I have not. Tell me, what is it?"

Lang explained all he knew, including their predicament.

Madam Desmona's hand dramatically flew to her heart. "How horrible. You poor boys, let me see those watches." She leaned forward and grasped Lang's watch in her hand. The orbs above trembled and the crow flapped its wings. She shook her head.

"There's more than this so-called Vytiper here, it feels like a forest entity. Powerful. But I'm afraid I can't help you."

"You can't see how to get them off?" Henry said.

She shook her head, but her eyes darted to a cabinet in the corner of the room. "Perhaps I know someone who would." She shuffled around the cabinet drawers, tossing out crystals and candles until she found a business card. "This is a friend of mine, Rodney Blackmore. He's an entity expert and he might be able to help you."

"Thank you so much," Henry said.

"Do let me know if everything works out. Oh, before you go, shall I take a peek at your palms?"

Henry tilted his head. "Why?"

Madam Desmona cackled a laugh. "To do a palm reading. A glimpse into your future."

"My future is on my palm?"

"Of course. Give me your hand." She took his hand into her strong, dry ones and traced the lines on his palm with a pointed fingernail. All the candles in the room flickered. "It seems you do have a shorter lifespan than most. Goodness, seven children? You're also a bit selfish when it comes to love."

Henry glanced at Lang.

"Lang, your turn." She squinted at the lines. "You're going to live a long life full of many romances." She wagged her finger and looked at him with flashing eyes. "You must not fall prey to the hopelessness of guilt. Watch out for truffles."

"Uh, thanks," Lang said.

"Boys, go now to your destinies."

They stepped out and took deep breaths of air that was not saturated with perfume.

"Watch out for truffles?" Lang said.

Henry shrugged and took a look at the business card. There was a phone number and a picture of a white ghost of the bedsheet variety. They walked to a payphone on the street corner and Henry dialed the number.

The phone rang.

And rang.

And rang.

He heard the receiver click, followed by silence.

"Uh, hello? Is anyone there?"

A raspy voice whispered from the receiver, "who calls Rodney Blackmore?"

"My name is Henry Bats, I got your number from Madam

Desmona. Me and my friend, Lang, need to talk to you about Vytipers."

There was a moment of silence.

"Hello?"

"459 Gurgle Way." The phone deadlined and Henry hung up.

"All he said was 459 Gurgle Way."

"That's near where I live," Lang said. "Follow me."

He led them to Quivery Quarters, a tangle of densely packed buildings that smelled vaguely like tomato sauce. Henry spied a rat assessing a dumpster, a cat assessing the rat, and what he swore was a shadow on the wall assessing them both. A man with a droopy hat was sitting on a stoop watching them walk by and he muttered something about Walpogs.

Lang plowed ahead, weaving this way and that through the streets and alleyways. Several lamps were out, making it even darker. They finally stopped at a shop tower connected by walkways and stairs. Beneath the shops was a shadowy underpass. Lang gestured to the entrance, the first few feet of the passageway visible in the murk.

"Look straight ahead, don't turn your head to the left or right. And whatever you do, don't turn back." Lang said.

"Why?"

"You'll see."

Henry tentatively took a step into the tunnel. As his eyes adjusted to the dark he could see a faint, quivering light in the distance. He focused on the light, took a deep breath, and made his feet shuffle forward. For the first few steps, there was silence. But soon a soft whisper tugged at his ear. Then a second whisper, and a third, until a mass of garbled voices surrounded his head and filled the tunnel. He hunched up his shoulders and grabbed on tight to his backpack straps. The voices got louder until the tunnel was a symphony of discordant wailing. Disoriented and dizzy, Henry stumbled and turned to catch himself against the clammy passage walls. Through the voice ruckus, he heard Lang shout, "Don't look!" He felt Lang's hand on his back, steadying him, and forced himself to keep moving, eyes focused on the light. They approached the end and the voices faded away. Henry could feel his head clear. They came out on the other side and he turned back to look. Empty silence.

"What was that?"

"Everyone calls it Howlers' Tunnel."

"I can see why."

"You're not supposed to look at the walls or you'll see faces. But when you have to walk through it every day, you get used to it. Come on, we're getting close."

House number 459 on Gurgle Way and the entire neighborhood was in need of repair. The clapboard panels on the house were skewed and rotted and the windows were boarded up. Henry stepped carefully to avoid fallen shingles from the roof and nearly two dozen ectolanterns that surrounded the property.

They stepped onto the creaky porch and Lang pushed the doorbell. They heard a chime begin on a pleasant note and end in an off-key screech. They waited a minute and rang the bell again.

Henry called through the door, "Mr Blackmore, this is Henry Bats and Langley Skullfield. Madam Desmona sent us, remember?"

Not a sound came from within the house. They were just about to leave when the door clicked and opened a crack.

"It's just you two?" said the same whisper Henry had heard on the phone.

"Yes," Lang said.

"You may enter in one minute. Lock the door behind you."

After one minute, they did as instructed. The house was dark. So dark, in fact, they couldn't see in front of them. Henry swayed uneasily. "Mr Blackmore?"

They heard a shuffle a good distance away.

"I'm here," Mr Blackmore whispered.

"Why is it so dark?" Lang said.

"They're attracted to the light."

"What are?"

"*Them.*"

"Oh."

They heard another noise, a bit closer. "You're having trouble with Vytipers?" Mr Blackmore's voice reminded Henry of something, but he couldn't figure out what.

"That's right," Lang said. "We helped them and now we're stuck with these time bombs."

"Never do as the non-human says."

"We learned our lesson, now we want to get these watches off."

There were two thumps, each from the opposite direction. Henry stepped closer to where he imagined Lang to be. "So could you help us?"

"Vytipers. Only encountered one, a shadow I caught prowling the streets. They're a fairly recent entity, you see, so they're quite rare and most aren't even aware of their existence. But I did manage to strike up a conversation. Learned an interesting fact, something not many experts know."

"What?"

"They used to be human. How the Vytiper went from human to what it was, I don't know."

"Before stealing part of our life, they made us stand on someone's grave. Maybe it was the grave of the person they used to be?" Lang said.

"I wouldn't be surprised."

Henry knew what it was about Mr Blackmore's voice that was bothering him. At times, it was similar to the Vytiper's voice, unearthly and muted. There was another shuffle only a few feet away and he took a step backwards. "Is there anything else, Mr Blackmore?"

"That's all I know."

"We'll be going then. Thanks for your help."

"Watch out for *them*."

Henry turned around and fumbled for the door lock. He found it and they both hurried outside.

"Did you get the feeling..." Lang said.

"That something wasn't right?" Henry finished.

They nodded in agreement and found themselves walking back towards Howlers' Tunnel. "So Greta Flingbossom and Jacoby Dread. That's who did this to us."

"Sounds like it," Lang said. "Now the question is why."

"I have to get home for dinner, but let's meet tomorrow. There's a restaurant I like called RIP. We could talk there after school."

"Sure."

They reached the entrance to Howlers' Tunnel. Henry looked through it nervously.

"Do you know your way home?" Lang said.

"I think so."

"I would recommend running through the tunnel. Plugging your ears helps a bit, but not much."

"Thanks." Henry waved goodbye, took a deep breath, and sprinted to the other side. Lang was right, it did help.

Chapter 3

Frank Loses a Cobalt Sidewinder

RIP stood for Refined Immortal Pasta. Henry wasn't sure what that meant, but the restaurant's food tasted good and that was all that mattered. The walls were the color of pesto and covered with paintings of every noodle imaginable, and the back of the booths was shaped like cushiony rigatoni.

"Never been here before," Lang said when the hostess seated them.

"I come with my family all the time."

The waiter, long and thin like spaghetti, smiled at them. "The usual, Henry?"

"Make it two, Farfallo." He fiddled with his napkin. "So we know Vytipers used to be human."

Lang nodded. "That means the grave next to Greta..." he trailed off and stared blankly.

"What about a grave?"

"Nothing. Just thinking. So why would they choose us?"

"I don't know. Reading Mrs Mutter's cases, it seems like they go with kids."

"I wonder if there's a way to find out more about Greta and Jacoby."

"There has to be information on dead people somewhere."

"That'd be the Hall of Records on Curdle Court."

Farfallo set down two plates of steaming lasagna slabs on the table.

"Thanks," Henry said and looked at Lang. "You got time to go to the Hall of Records after this?"

"Let's do it."

The two ate every last bite of their food and ordered a Cobweb

Cake slice for dessert. With full bellies, they found their way to the Hall of Records, a gray building with equally gray people inside it. The front desk was manned by a woman with a stern facial expression. She spoke as though her nose was pinched. "May I help you?"

Henry stepped forward. "Hi, we were wondering if we could see some records. Death records, to be specific."

"All death records are available to the public. Tell me the names."

"Jacoby Dread and Greta Flingbossom."

"One moment."

She disappeared through a door behind the counter and a few minutes later reappeared with two files. Henry took the one for Jacoby Dread and gulped. He carefully opened the file to a single paper inside that revealed Dread's birth and death date, the cause of death (Cellar Fever), and a black and white photograph of Jacoby himself, in which he wore a bowler hat and a pinstripe suit. He looked to be in his 50s with a light blond mustache curled at the ends, a solemn frown, and dark, sunken eyes that stared directly at the camera. He was posed with a cane in his hand. Henry looked at Lang's file and saw that Greta Flingbossom was younger with light hair and an equally somber expression. She sat in a chair and wore a long, lavishly decorated gown.

"Do you have more information from when they were living?" Lang said.

"Not that you can see." The lady snatched the files back.

The two looked at each other and dejectedly left the hall of records. Outside, Lang sighed. "Guess that's it then. Another dead end."

"For now," Henry said. "If you think of anything, call." They exchanged phone numbers and parted ways.

Henry was too lost in thought to glance at the worm lady when he passed by her house and barely noticed the gooey pink concoction Mildred served when he sat down for dinner. Hattie snapped him out of it when she pointed at his neck. "What's that?"

He looked down to find the pocket watch had somehow made its way over his shirt. He choked on the goo spoonful he was about to swallow. Mildred paused her ladling, Gobbert stopped mid-bite of a charred biscuit piece, and Grandpa Flemm stared with narrowed eyes. Henry said the first thing he could think of. "Uh, I traded a comic for it with a boy at school."

"But what is it?" Hattie asked.

"A pocket watch."

Flemm smacked his fist on the table causing goo to jump from the bowls. "Pocket watch. We had those in the war."

"You didn't have wristwatches?" Henry said, trying to divert attention.

"No wrist. Only pocket."

"But why do you need a pocket watch, Hen?" Mildred asked.

"Well, you know how I'm always late to things."

"You seem punctual to me."

"And who's this boy you're talking about?" said Gobbert.

"Langley Skullfield. He has one too."

Mildred clapped her hands together. "You made a friend? We have to invite him over."

"But Mom-"

"Tomorrow for dinner." She stood up and searched around the messy counter. "Where's a notepad? I have to make a grocery list."

"I really don't think-"

"Have him check with his parents. Oh, this will be so much fun."

Henry shifted his weight back and forth on the school steps and hiked his backpack on his shoulder. When he saw Lang, he waved him over. "Hey." He stared at the ground and shuffled his feet. "Are you busy tonight?"

"Why? Did you think of something we can do?" Lang held the slightest hint of hopeful enthusiasm in his eyes.

"No. Actually, I ended up telling my family about you. Don't worry, they don't know the real story behind the pocket watches, but my mom wants you to come over for dinner."

The enthusiasm disappeared. "I don't think so."

"But the thing is, well, she's really looking forward to it. I think she's buying like five bags of groceries."

Lang glanced to the side. "Tonight?"

"Yeah."

"If she already bought the stuff, I guess I could go."

"Okay, it'll be alright, promise."

Lang nodded and walked silently with Henry to his house. They opened the door to a waft of mingled spices and rich scents. The kitchen was spotless, even the sludge on the backsplash was gone. A green and black checked cloth was on the table and the silverware was perfectly aligned with the plates.

"It's nice," Lang whispered and straightened out the gray sweatshirt he wore.

"It's not usually like this," Henry said, stunned.

Mildred, who was stirring something on the stove, turned around at their voices. "The boys are here," she called into the living room. "You must be Langley. I'm Mildred, Henry's mom." She extended her hand and Lang shook it.

Gobbert and Hattie entered and introductions were made.

"You can just call me Lang," he said.

"Of course, Lang," she said, pulling out a chair for him. "Please sit. Hattie, get your grandfather."

"But it's Henry's turn."

"Henry has a guest. Now go, dear."

Hattie rolled her eyes and stomped upstairs. Henry sat next to Lang while Mildred served the food.

"Beef casserole, fried zucchini, and bread rolls. For dessert, we're having chocolate cake."

"Not bad," said Henry.

Flemm and Hattie came in and sat in their usual chairs. "Who's this?" Flemm squinted at the boy.

"This is Henry's friend, Lang."

"Lang. Sounds like a type of lettuce. In the war-"

"Please ignore him," Mildred said, blushing. "And please, eat."

Hattie leaned across the table with her chin in her hands. "How old are you?"

"Fourteen."

"Wow. Do you know much about the other regions? We learned about their economic systems in school today."

"I'm familiar."

"The Botsworth Trams are the only way to get stuff back and forth. I really want to go to the Umbra Region. Lots of Nightspooks there. You have a pocket watch just like Henry. Do you like wolves?"

"They're alright."

"Do you want to see my doll collection after dinner?"

"No one cares about your dolls," Henry said.

"You can show me," said Lang.

Hattie stuck her tongue out at her brother.

The casserole was perfectly cooked, the zucchini was seasoned just right, and rolls didn't have too much butter on them.

"Did you follow a recipe, Mom?" Henry asked.

"I thought I'd try a few things out from your great-aunt Gertrude. Of course, nothing beats the way I whip things up in the kitchen."

Henry and Hattie raised their eyebrows.

"Nothing beats a good bowl of lettuce," Flemm added.

After a bombardment of questions throughout the rest of the meal, Hattie grabbed Lang by the hand and dragged him to her room. Henry followed with folded arms.

"That's Matilda and Yvette and Isadora and Edwina and Sydney and Louis. I used to be able to do tricks with a Nightspook, but it disappeared. Oh, and this is Cassidy, Loretta, Timothea, and-"

"I think he's had enough, Hattie," Henry said, stepping in.

"Oh, all right. Which one is your favorite?" She looked at Lang with shining eyes.

He shrugged. "Isadora?"

Hattie nodded approvingly. "She's wonderful, one of my favorites."

"They're all your favorite," Henry said.

"Wrong. I'm not particularly fond of Gretchen."

Mildred popped in. "Lang, would you like to stay for television?"

"Sure."

They all sat squished on the orange couch, Lang tucked in between Henry and Hattie, who insisted on being next to the guest. They watched the news, which reported on the spread of the Walpog outbreak. Gobbert got up every so often to adjust the rabbit ears when the reception went bad. When the news was over, Lang said he was expected home soon and they gathered around the door to say goodbye.

"Please come again, it was lovely meeting you," Mildred said.

"I'm sure I'll have new dolls to show you next time," said Hattie.

"Oh, before you go," Gobbert reached into his pocket, "take these for the road." He handed him a few Bone Crusher packets, sugar teeth that were the latest development at Gelatin Skeleton.

"Thanks, Mr Bats."

Henry walked out with him. "Sorry about Hattie, she's a pest."

Lang bent his head to the ground. "It's fine."

"You weren't bothered much?"

"Not really."

"Well, I'll see you later. And don't worry. We'll figure out how to get these watches off."

"See you."

Henry watched Lang walk away with his hands in his pockets. Back inside, Mildred raved about Henry's new friend, Hattie equally taken.

Class the next day dragged on forever. Mrs Squid was going on and on about the history of Granville Botsworth, but Henry could only focus on his impending death. He tried to push the thought out, but it stayed put. If he had less than ten years to live, what would he do with his life? He could do nothing, of course, and proceed as normal. Or, he could do everything. Collect as many comic books as possible, travel to the other Regions, start his own Peculiar Pet empire, spend more time with Corn Chip.

"Mr Bats, would you care to share your current thoughts with the class?" Mrs Squid hovered above him, mouth anchored into a frown. His classmate's eyes were on him.

"Um, just thinking about the future."

"And what would that entail?"

"Corn Chip."

The class snickered.

"Mr Bats, I suggest you put more focus on the great Granville Botsworth and less on food products."

"Yes, Mrs Squid."

With Lang nowhere to be found after school, Henry decided a trip to Frank's was in order. He found the owner underneath his desk with a flashlight, muttering to himself.

"Frank?" Henry kneeled down beside him.

"Ah, Henry. The Cobalt Sidewinder got loose. Help me find it, will ya? Here's a flashlight. And careful, she bites."

Henry got onto his hands and knees and crawled on the tiled floor, peeking beneath tanks and shelving units. He was halfway underneath a toad tank stack when the door jingled.

"Do you have Torpedo Sharks?" asked a formal male voice.

"Right over here."

Henry listened to Frank and the customer walk over to the aquatic section.

"How many you want?"

"One for today. I'm just starting up my shark tank again."

Henry spotted a wriggle of cobalt in the flashlight shine. "Found her," he called.

"See if you can get her out," Frank called back. "Remember when we wrangled that Fogmouth? Use the same technique."

Henry pushed himself further under the shelf and became as still as possible, preparing to grab the snake's tail.

"That'll be 78," Frank said. "What did you say your name was?"

"I didn't say. But it's Jacoby Dread."

The words startled Henry so much, he jerked his head up and smacked it on the metal shelf.

"Did she get you, Henry?" Frank said.

He slid out from underneath the shelf just in time to see the man leave the store. He was wearing a bowler hat.

Chapter 4

Dread Manor's Secret

"I forgot I need to do something." Henry shoved the flashlight into Frank's hands and rushed out the door.

"Thanks for finding the Sidewinder," Frank yelled sarcastically.

Down the street to the left was the man with the bowler hat. Henry walked after him, his heart pumping with the idea of coming face to face with the person who could very well be Jacoby Dread. He weaved between crowds on the sidewalk, eyes glued to the bowler hat. Just when he was close enough to reach out and grab the man's green pea coat, he veered to the right and entered a tavern called The Stout Fish. Henry gathered all his courage and went in after him. It was dark and hazy and the smell reminded him of Grandpa Flemm's attic.

"No children. Can't you read?" The man at the bar pointed to a sign on the door.

"This'll just take a minute."

Henry scanned the room and his eyes landed on the face from the death record - Jacoby Dread, blond mustache, bowler hat and all. He sat in a lonely corner booth, the small Torpedo Shark swimming back and forth in the container on the table. Before the bartender could stop him, Henry took a deep breath and marched forward. He sat firmly in the seat across from the man, who looked up from his drink menu. His blank expression was dotted with two sharp, watery eyes, which stayed unchanged as they focused on the boy before him.

"I see I have a visitor." His voice was clipped and tired, his face equally so.

"Do you know who I am?"

"Henry Bats, what a surprise."

"You're Jacoby Dread?"

He looked down at the menu. "Well done. Yes, I am."

In his search for words, Henry found himself tongue-tied.

"By your presence here, I assume you understand the meaning of that watch around your neck."

Henry nodded.

"Unfortunately, there's nothing I can do about it."

Anger rose in the pit of Henry's stomach. "Is that so?"

"Indeed."

"You don't care at all that I'll die in ten years because of you?"

Jacoby let out a long sigh and fiddled with gold rings on his right hand, his left hand gloved. "Death is a terrible thing, and life can be so unforgiving. I only did what I had to do to keep what's mine."

"At the cost of my life."

"I was originally going to choose Hattie. I spotted her walking down the street in search of a catalyst. But I grew a fondness for her." His mouth upturned slightly at the thought. "How is she? Any new dolls?"

Henry gritted his teeth. "She's fine."

"Very good. Now, I suspect you won't leave me alone after our little meeting here, the last one didn't."

"There was someone before me?"

"Yes, unfortunately, the lifespan I gained from him was rather short, thus I've already suffered two deaths in my time."

"How unfortunate."

"As I know you'll continue to seek me, I'll save you the trouble, plus I'd like to see Hattie again. I live in the Manor at the end of Sable Avenue. But hear me now, you won't find anything of interest." He picked up the shark and stood up. "I'm afraid I've lost my thirst. I'll be seeing you, Henry Bats."

Jacoby Dread left the tavern.

"Out," the bartender motioned with his thumb.

Henry's mind flooded with a hundred things he could have

said or done, and he stomped outside.

"Greedy... lousy... selfish... life stealer." He found a lamppost and kicked it, hard. The pain sent him hopping on one foot. "Ow, ow, ow."

His hopping slowed to a stop when a familiar face caught his eye from across the street. Amongst a small group of boys and girls was Hattie, and she was looking right back at him. She ducked behind two girls and the group scurried away down a side street.

"What's she up to?" Henry said, limping back home.

Hattie was absent from dinner that night. According to Gobbert, she was volunteering for the library again for extra credit, but Henry believed none of it. He was in the middle of math homework when he heard her come home, and he stepped into the hallway with his arms folded. She stopped when she saw him.

"Have a nice time at the *library*?" He said.

She folded her arms back. "I did. Did you have a nice time at the *tavern*?"

"I wasn't at a tavern."

"I watched you leave The Stout Fish and kick a lamppost."

"So you admit you weren't at the library?"

She delicately adjusted the bow in her hair. "I was on my way."

"Pretty sure the library is in the opposite direction. And who were all those kids?"

"None of your business."

"Want to make it Mom and Dad's business?"

"Want me to tell them you were at a bar?"

Henry glared at her and considered the consequences. "Fine. Forget everything we saw?"

"Deal."

Henry flagged Lang down after school the next day and

relayed his chance encounter with Jacoby Dread. Lang listened, shocked.

"So Greta's out there somewhere," he said, gazing into the distance. "I can't believe you saw Jacoby in person. He said there was nothing he could do?"

"Yep. But I'm betting there is. And I just let him walk away."

"He told you where he lived, didn't he?"

"You think it was the truth?

Lang directed himself toward the cemetery. "There's only one way to find out."

Henry nodded. "The manor at the end of Sable Avenue."

They walked in stride. The air was crisp and breezy and Henry could smell rain coming. They passed by the Sable Avenue cemetery and continued down the street. Imposing gates and brick fences concealed the residences, and the sidewalk turned from concrete to stone. The street ended at a black, wrought iron gate that looked like a prison guard. 'Dread Manor' was spelled out with twisted iron bars, which Lang easily pushed open to reveal a five-story, dreary mansion.

Henry's mouth fell open. Its gray stone walls were ensnared by creeping vines and framed by leafless, bony trees. A driveway circled a fountain with a fat cherub spouting greenish water, and a brick wall barricaded the property just before the forest began. "There are places like this in the Penumbra Region?" Henry asked, eyes taking in the scene.

"Guess so. This must have cost a fortune, it takes up so much space."

They walked forward, the grounds lit by posts topped with orbs emanating a green light. The entrance to the Manor had double doors with looped shark knockers. Henry pounded them three times. It was immediately opened by a tall, elderly butler wearing a gray suit and a plain expression. His nose took up the majority of his face and overshadowed sunken, lifeless eyes.

"Dread Residence. Who calls?" he said in a dull tone.

"I'm Henry Bats, here to see Jacoby Dread. This is my friend, Lang."

"Master Dread has been expecting you. Right this way."

They were led up three flights of stairs and through hallways with stone floors and deep red walls. Henry looked up at portraits of men in bowler hats and women in feathered ones. Empty pedestals were covered with a thin dust layer and half burnt candles that lit the way.

Their footsteps echoed through the massive, barren manor until they came to a door set with two of the largest portraits above them. They were of similar-looking men facing each other, one with a deep frown, the other neutral. They shared Jacoby's light hair and dark eyes.

"Mr Dread is in his study."

Ferdinand opened the doors and Henry found Jacoby busily sorting through a paper stack on his desk. A giant fish tank in the back of the room contained the single Torpedo Shark. Hundreds of books lined the walls from top to bottom.

Jacoby didn't even bother to look up. "Henry, come so soon?"

"I brought my friend, Lang. A Vytiper stole his life too."

"Greta Flingbossom," Lang added, exposing the pocket watch from underneath his shirt, the gold gleaming in the dim light.

"Never heard of her. Now, what do you want?"

"We want to know how you became a Vytiper," Henry said.

Dread put up a finger and wagged it. "Ah, ah, that's a secret."

"Why?"

"It won't do you any good to know."

"Tell us anyway."

"If you've only come to pester me about this topic, I'm afraid you won't get anywhere. Besides, I have work to do." He sat back in his chair and rubbed his temples. "It's a great hassle, Henry, to come back to life. So many things have to be sorted through all over again. And Ferdinand is only useful for shuffling about the manor." He gestured toward the door where the butler had disappeared. Dread grunted and picked up a heavy brass stamp with his gloved left hand. "You've come to my house, you know there's nothing more I can offer you. Be good boys and end it here. Ferdinand has something for you in the hall, now be gone." He waved his right hand in dismissal and with a flourish stamped the documents that lay on his desk.

"But, please-" Henry began.

"Go, or Ferdinand will remove you."

Henry stomped his foot in frustration and left the study with Lang. In the hallway, Ferdinand was indeed holding a small satin pouch. He dropped it into Henry's hand and escorted the boys back through the maze of corridors and out to the driveway.

Henry felt the pouch weight in his hand, its contents making a muffled clinking. "Should I look?"

Lang nodded and Henry cautiously pulled the string tied around it. Lang leaned in. "What is it?"

Henry shook his head. "Money. He's trying to bribe me to stop bothering him. He thinks this isn't a big deal." He gripped the pouch in his fist and chucked it into the cherub fountain. It splashed and sank to the murky bottom. "But if we don't stop him, how many more people is he going to do this to? And you only have a few weeks to live. We have to fix this."

They walked through the gate and started back down the stone sidewalk.

"You know, there must be a reason he won't tell us how he became a Vytiper."

"You're right."

Lang continued, "This might be a stupid idea, but maybe there's something in his mansion? I think he and Ferdinand are the only people there, it shouldn't be too hard to sneak in. I mean, the gate wasn't even locked."

Henry considered the idea of entering the mansion undetected and navigating the maze-like interior looking for... he didn't even know what.

"Hate to say it, but it's probably our best shot."

"When should we go?"

"The sooner the better. Tonight at midnight?"

"Tonight at midnight."

As soon as Henry's alarm clock ticked to 11:40 pm, he peeled off his blanket and changed out of his pajamas. He opened his door as quietly as possible and tiptoed out through Gobbert's snoring. From a drawer in the kitchen, he fished out a flashlight and stuck it in his school backpack. Prepared to leave, he unlocked the front door and gently closed it behind him. It was raining. The streets were flooded with water, reflecting the glowing lampposts. There was no sign of human life except a few cars with bright headlights that splashed through the streets. Shadows and Ghasts flitted in and out of his vision. The rain brought them out like earthworms.

Henry wiped water from his eyes, his sweatshirt already drenched. He arrived at the mansion gate to find a soaked-through Lang. The wind picked up and whipped through the creaky trees that surrounded the manor. A thunderclap shook the sky and made them jump.

"Are you ready?" whispered Henry.

Lang nodded. "Are you?"

"Yeah," he gulped.

They pushed the gate open and, moving from shadow to shadow of the green orbs, approached the front door. Henry quietly tried the handle, but it was locked. Sticking close to the cold, wet exterior, they made their way to the side of the manor. The first floor was lined with windows, their frames flaking black paint. The boys had to stand on their tip-toes to reach the bottom of the windowsills. Whether they were locked or just stuck, the windows wouldn't budge. Henry tried the last window with little hope, but there was just a hint of give under his palm. He took a deep breath and pushed hard with all his strength, and the window slid with just enough space for the boys to slip through.

"You first," Lang said.

The taller boy boosted Henry up and through the open window. Henry turned around and grabbed Lang's arms, pulling him through. They were in a room with a dining table covered by a white tablecloth that rippled from the wind. Henry closed the window and the sudden stillness of the house pressed in on them. They crept into the hallway, leaving a trail of water behind. A few candles flickered light onto suits of armor that lined the edge of the hall. The mansion structure creaked and popped from the wind and cold of the rain.

"What exactly are we looking for?" Henry whispered.

"I don't know. I think we should go back to his office."

Henry nodded in agreement and they continued past the rows of armor and up the main staircase. On the third floor, there were even more. "Lang, do you remember seeing these earlier?"

"No. He must have put them up after we left."

Henry stared into the pitch black helmets, half expecting them to turn and look back.

"Was it here, or straight?" he asked when they came to a fork.

"Straight, I think I remember that portrait."

The eyes of the paintings watched them sneak by and Henry

couldn't help but look over his shoulder. After several more forks and a bit of backtracking, they arrived at the double doors. Lang opened them a crack and peeked through. "All clear."

Lang headed to the bookshelves, Henry to Jacoby's desk. Lightning flashed through the window behind the aquarium, illuminating the lonely Torpedo Shark. Henry searched through folders and drawers with his flashlight and found a list titled To-Do. It read:

-Contact Punge Domestic Agency
-See if Chef Morose is available
-Organize Return Ball
-Bank accounts in order
-Manage assets
-Move everything from basement
-Awaken Ferdinand
-Replenish shark tank
-Tea party?

He flipped through several financial reports and business-type folders until Lang called him over. He held worn, stained sheets of paper.

"What's that?"

"Grayprints of the mansion, they show all the rooms. I found them folded between some books."

They studied the intricate drawings – the upper floors, the basement, the office they were in, and finally the first floor. "This is weird." Lang pointed to a large room at the back of the mansion labeled 'Conservatory.' A line was drawn from the conservatory to the page bottom, where another room was labeled 'Arcanum.'

"It seems like this room is separate from the mansion, but the line might mean there's a way to get in from the Conservatory."

Henry's eyes widened. "A secret room?"

"I think so."

They looked at each other and nodded. Using the grayprints to navigate, they tiptoed back downstairs and zigzagged through hallways until they came to the metal conservatory door. It opened with a slow, searing screech to reveal the dark glass house. Outside, the storm had intensified. Every lightning flash lit the room like fire. Rain battered against the glass with a deafening roar. They took out their flashlights and made their way through tangled, overgrown plants and twitching weeds. A particular bunch of Carnivorous Chokeberries twisted their stems as they passed, the scent of mildew and dirt filling their noses.

"Now what?" Henry said.

"Look for some kind of passageway."

Henry shone the flashlight to the mossy floor, hoping to find a trap door. "This could take a while." The path he was on brought him to the conservatory center, where a gray Umbra Flytrap statue stood a little taller than himself. Etched onto a plaque were the words:

The hungry creepers awaken from sleep,
Not with light, but flies and meat
To reveal their fruit from the earthy deep.

Henry stared at the inscription. "Fruit from the deep," he said to himself. "Instructions? Creepers eating meat, that has to be the flytraps." He inspected the statue, his hand grazing the pointed marble teeth edged along two open leaves ready to snap. "But which flytraps?"

On a hunch, he rested his forearm on the length of the bottom leaf and pressed down. The top leaf fell and jabbed Henry's skin with its points. "Ouch." He pulled his arm out while the leaves slowly returned to their original position.

"Over here!" Lang called.

Henry followed his voice to the back of the glass house. Lang was standing in front of an old fountain filled with thick, algae-ridden water. A flytrap statue much larger than the other was resting its head on the sludge. Its leaves were open to reveal a staircase carved into the bottom.

"It just opened," Lang said. "Hey, what are those marks on your arm?"

"Tell you later," Henry said and put his attention on the sunken staircase. "Well, we found it."

"Now we have to go down it."

He stared at the black abyss that awaited them. "You first this time."

Lang wielded his flashlight. He stepped onto the fountain ledge and hopped onto the stone leaf, setting his feet down the steps one at a time. Henry followed close behind until they reached the bottom. It was strangely quiet, a stark contrast to the stormy symphony of the conservatory. As they reached the bottom steps, through the light of their flashlights, they discovered what lay in the secret room. It was a sort of laboratory. Scorched tables were covered with tubes and beakers and scattered with books and papers. Jars were filled with liquid and bits and parts of things that were only identifiable by their labels. Henry put his hand on the cave-like walls carved out from the stony underground. The pickle-like formaldehyde smell was overwhelming.

"Wow," Henry said, his voice strange and loud in the silence.

Lang scanned through the jars. "Liquid Quartz, Preserved Mole Fingers, Essence of Walpog."

"How do you get an essence?"

"I'd rather not find out."

Henry sorted through worn and stained books, most handwritten in a language he didn't recognize. He plunked a heavy leather bound one in the table center and cracked it open. Its contents were made up of symbols and illustrations, but one page, in particular, made him stop. It was a pencil drawing of a pocket watch with a tiger in the middle.

"Lang, here."

Lang put down the lab equipment he was inspecting and stared at the illustration alongside Henry. "I think we found what we're looking for."

The next page depicted the dial at the top the watch being pulled up and twisted off to reveal a small compartment.

"I never thought of that," Lang said. He gave his flashlight to Henry, held up his watch, and pulled the dial up. After much twisting, it did indeed come off to reveal an empty cavity. Lang screwed the dial back on.

"You aren't allowed down here."

Chills ran up and down Henry's back, and he whirled around. Ferdinand was standing in front of the staircase, his tall figure and expressionless face barely visible in the light.

Chapter 5

Grigory Chim and His Clocks

"You will come with me," Ferdinand said and strode towards the boys.

Heart beating wildly, Henry did the only thing he could think. He switched off the flashlights. His hands scrambled on the table for the book and once it was in his grasp he shouted, "Lang, run."

Henry plowed forward, envisioning where the stairs were in the darkness. As he reached the first step, a body brushed against his arm and cold, bony fingers snatched at his neck. In a flood of energy, he darted up the stairs. Once in the conservatory, he made himself stop to wait for Lang. He heard footsteps and spotted the outline of Lang in the darkness. The two sprinted into the hallway, not daring to look back until they found the front door. Hands trembling, Henry threw open the bolt and burst out into the rain. They passed the overflowing cherub fountain, its smile twisted in a lightning flash. They ran through the iron gate and back onto the streets. Near the cemetery, they stopped to catch their breath, Henry still clutching the book to his chest.

"You alright?" Lang said, wiping away water from his face.

"I think so," Henry said in-between breaths.

"You got the book?"

He held it out. "Got it."

"It looked like it was in some sort of code, or language we could translate. We'll need help. 11 o'clock tomorrow at Botsworth Library?"

"Let's do it. But Lang, he knows where I live. He'll see it's missing and come after me."

"I'll take it for the night. You just remember to lock your door."

Henry handed him the book and smiled. "We're actually getting somewhere."

"Looks like it."

Henry hurried home, glancing over his shoulder every block, half expecting to see Ferdinand's sunken eyes and ashen face behind him. Once he was home he locked the doors, and despite worries of a visit from the residents of Dread Manor, fell asleep as soon as his head hit the pillow.

It was almost nine when Henry woke up, glad it was the weekend, and that he didn't find Ferdinand hovering over his bed looking for the stolen book. He was, however, not happy to find a Thread-Spinner had made its rounds through the house during the night. When he grabbed his blanket to throw it off, he also grabbed a handful of sticky, black thread.

"Great," he said, hopping between carpet patches that weren't crisscrossed with string. He quickly dressed and went downstairs to eat breakfast.

Hattie was in the living room watching cartoons, Grandpa Flemm eating a mush bowl beside her. Henry joined them with a bowl of Sugar Slugs. "Where's Mom and Dad?"

"They went to get Thread-Spinner Spray," she said. They were halfway through a show when she spoke up again. "I know you snuck out last night."

"Sneaking," Grandpa Flemm mumbled.

Henry kept eating his slugs, eyes glued to the TV. "Prove it."

"I heard you come home at... let's see, one in the morning? Two?"

He shrugged. "No idea what you're talking about."

"I'm going to figure out what you were doing, and when I do, you'll be sorry." She sat back on the couch, pleased with her declaration.

"It's not like I'm the only one. Last week you were supposed to be volunteering for the library, remember?" Before she had time to retort, he jumped up from the couch and grabbed his backpack. "Gotta go."

"Bring back lettuce," Grandpa Flemm shouted after him.

The streets of Grimworld were still wet from the rain, but clear of fog. Henry decided to wait at a GrimBus Stop for a bus that would take him to Botsworth Library on the other side of the Penumbra Region. Soon, a GrimBus barreled towards him. It was big and purple and barely fit on the road. Its red headlights cut through the gloom and nearly blinded Henry. Stopping with a screech, the shriveled old driver opened the doors. Henry gave him the bus fare and took a seat in the middle. A short lady with a puff of red hair tied with a handkerchief scurried on board and took the seat behind him. The GrimBus jerked and chugged along, Henry exiting when the driver announced his stop. He scurried off and headed for his destination.

Botsworth Library was the largest in the region and stood tallest amongst a knot of buildings and busy trams. The outside was ringed with tall, stone columns and crowned with an enormous dome. Inside were endless rows of books and dim reading nooks containing tables and chairs. Henry found Lang in one such nook sitting in a chair encircled by stacks of old, leather-bound volumes.

"Anything happen at your house?" Lang asked.

"Nope."

"Good." He motioned to the books surrounding him. "These are all on decoding. I'm pretty sure the Dread book isn't in another language, it's a cryptogram."

"A code? Great, weekend homework."

"It shouldn't be that hard. See, I think this little squiggle here is an 'e.'" He pointed in the book. "And this one might be 'l.' We just need to narrow down the others from here."

Hours later they sat collapsed on the floor, paper and pencils borrowed from the library strewn about them, the decoding attempts in front of Henry blurring in and out of focus. "Nothing makes sense anymore."

Lang held his head in his hand, furiously scribbling notes. "I keep thinking I'm getting somewhere, but it's always a dead end."

"All I know is, the one that looks like a spoon isn't an 'a.'"

"Are you sure? I've been using it as 'a' this whole time."

Henry groaned and dropped his pencil. "My brain hurts. Maybe we should give up for today."

"Giving up already?" The voice was familiar, and Henry looked up to see the lady with the curly red hair from the bus standing over him, holding a piece of paper. Only now he could see the blonde streaks that poked out from beneath the handkerchief.

"Hattie?"

She pulled off the red wig. "I followed you on the bus."

"Why?"

She ignored him and turned to Lang. "Hello Lang, good to see you again."

"Hello, Hattie."

Henry jumped to his feet. "Answer the question."

"I wanted to see what you were up to."

"We're just doing homework."

She raised her eyebrows. "I've been looking at your 'homework' all day and you haven't even noticed. No homework is that interesting. Cracking some kind of code, huh?"

"None of your business."

"Really? I guess you don't want the solution then."

"What do you mean?"

"The code for your little book." She held up the paper.

"You figured it out?"

"Yep."

Henry and Lang looked at each other.

"Of course, you're not getting it for free."

Henry made a move to snatch the paper from her hand, but she stepped back. "Too slow."

"Fine," he said, "first prove you've actually cracked it."

"Alright, here's some I translated." She cleared her throat and read from the paper, "You must select the image of an animal for the watchmaker. I've chosen a badger, as I feel this will personalize the watch to my character, and-"

"Okay, I believe you. Name your price."

"First, you have to get Grandpa for breakfast and dinner for the next two months."

Henry crossed his arms. "Fine."

"And second, as you're aware, my outings to the library aren't quite, er, what they seem. So you have to promise you won't tell Mom and Dad."

"Deal." He grabbed the paper. "Lang, let's go."

"You're not going to tell me what this is about?"

The boys grabbed the book and made for the exit. "Nope."

"Hey, wait!" By the time Hattie finished speaking, they were already gone.

"Now where?" Henry said.

"We could go to my house to translate it. My dad won't be home."

They took the GrimBus to Quivery Quarters and Lang led the way through Howlers' Tunnel to his apartment. It was on the sixth floor of a complex interlocked and meshed with the surrounding buildings. The stairwell was caked with a grime layer and the lightbulbs that hung from the ceiling flickered on and off. Televisions and music were blasting through thin walls, and the sour tomato smell was tingling Henry's nose.

Lang unlocked the door to his apartment. Henry craned his neck, curious as to what he would find. The space was simple and clean. The orange painted walls were empty of family photos or paintings, and the only furniture was a multi-colored, striped couch and TV. They went to Lang's room, equally simple with a desk and bunkbed. He took out paper and pencils and they started to work in silence. Lang started using the code from

Hattie to translate the right side of the book, Henry the left. But Henry wasn't thinking about the words being scratched out from his pencil.

"Where's your dad?" he asked.

"He works at the gas station on the weekends."

"Your mom?"

"Gone."

Henry paused in his translating. "Oh."

They continued working. Flipping a page in the book, Henry asked "So before, you talked about someone that had the pocket watch too. Who was he?"

"His name was Harlan."

"Did you know him well?"

Lang didn't look up from his writing. "He was my brother."

"Your brother?" Henry's pencil fell from his hand.

"Two Vytipers visited us on the same night. Now I know for sure they were Greta and Cloyd Flingbossom. We learned what the watches meant from the library and did everything we could to get them off, but we never figured out how. Then it was too late and he died from 'an unknown cause'."

Dropping his eyes to the paper, Henry whispered the only thing he could think to say, "Sorry."

Shrugging, Lang said. "It's not your fault."

Working in heavy silence, the handwriting in the book finally stopped. Lang organized the pages they had translated, and Henry read out loud, "*In my studies on immortality I have discovered a way in which one can live forever. Upon death, a human will transform into an entity I have named the Vytiper, through which they may possess their human form again. Vytipers do not age and cannot be killed by regular means.*

To become a Vytiper is as follows:

1. Assemble a pocket watch to exact specifications (page 34). This will most likely require the work of a watchmaker.

2. Acquire your ingredient list for the Vytiper's serum. A visit

to the GrimMan is necessary, as each concoction is different."

Henry looked up. "The GrimMan? Isn't that just a legend?"

"Guess not," Lang said.

He continued,

3. *Once you have the completed serum, pour the contents into the watch compartment. This will secure your fate as a Vytiper upon death.*

4. It is recommended that you now place the watch near your burial site for easy access.

5. Die.

6. You will now be in the Vytiper shadow form. Beware, it is a bit foggy. You must now locate, if you haven't already, a person in which you will take life. Children are recommended for their gullibility and amount of available lifespan.

7. Near your gravesite, have the chosen person locate the watch and turn to twelve o'clock.

8. Congratulations! You will soon wake up once again in your human body. You will be able to indicate the length of your lifespan by the watch, which will have been transferred to the chosen person. Each minute will represent one year of gained life until you reach the remaining number on the watch. The amount you acquire is random.

9. Repeat this process with the same watch and serum indefinitely.

The next line was written in a different color ink. *"Important note: the item discovered upon waking up must be concealed at all costs."*

The remaining book pages were blank, and Lang scanned through to ensure they didn't miss anything. "Wait a minute," he said. "There's a note hidden here."

The writing was in their regular language, tucked into the dip of two blank pages. It was in a different, hurried handwriting. Lang read, *"To undo: Speak with the GrimMan."*

Henry snapped his fingers. "So there is a way."

"The GrimMan is a powerful entity, right?"

"Yeah, but you know where this supposed GrimMan lives, don't you?"

"The forest," they said together.

Henry recalled a childhood rhyme:

A walk through the forest, dark and deep,
Where shadows and ghouls all slyly creep.
If you have a task that must be done,
There is someone for you, the only one.
Call to the GrimMan just but thrice,
With the plunk of music, you'll know he's arrived.
Be wary his tricks, or be eaten alive,
For the GrimMan loves to play with lives.

"You know that song about the GrimMan?"

"Yeah," said Lang, who had been thinking the same thing.

"Remember how it says he'll eat you alive?"

"Yep."

"You know we'll have to go anyway, right?"

"Uh huh." Lang stood up. "We're going to die sooner or later. But there's something I want to do first." He ran to the kitchen and came back with the Gray Pages. He flipped through and pointed to a listing titled 'Chim Chime.'

"The book says you need someone to make the pocket watch. Well, according to this, Chim Chime is the only watchmaker in the Penumbra Region. Maybe we should pay them a visit."

Henry grinned. "Genius. Maybe they'll know something about Greta Flingbossom."

"We'll need to take the GrimBus again."

"At least Hattie won't follow us."

The bumpy, rickety GrimBus made its way down the street, Henry and Lang seated in the front.

"Do you think Jacoby was the one who wrote the book?" Henry said.

"It's possible. The important thing is we know how Vytipers became what they are."

"And that there might be a way to undo it."

The bus dropped them off at a busy shopping intersection and they easily found Chim Chime, distinguished by a giant clock above the shop's door. Inside, they were met with the head-pounding tick of hundreds of clocks, all in perfect sync. The walls were plastered with every kind, from little baby clocks, tiny as a thumbnail, to great grandfathers with swaying pendulums. They went up to the glass counter, which contained wristwatches, stopwatches, and pocket watches, and Henry pushed the bell on the counter. They heard a clatter from the back room, followed by the arrival of a young man covered with clocks that were swinging around his neck as he pranced towards them. His shiny blonde hair swept and smoothed around his head and his bright eyes dazzled behind a pair of cog glasses. He wore a trim brown suit.

"Grigory Chim here, watchmaker extraordinaire," he said and shook their hands with gusto. "How may I be of service on this fine, gray day?"

"We were hoping you could-"

Grigory Chim held up his hand. "Shh, wait a second."

In exactly one second, the many clocks surrounding the trio all at once turned their hands to four o'clock. A burst of chimes, jingles, bells, and music nearly shook the floor they stood on. Cuckoo birds began popping out of their homes and a music chorus filled the room. Grigory looked around in bliss, Henry and Lang clapping their hands to their ears.

As the last booming chime drifted off, the watchmaker looked at them with his glistening eyes. "Beautiful, isn't it?"

The boys half-heartedly nodded.

"So, how can I be of help?"

Pulling out the pocket watches from their sweatshirts, ears ringing, Lang said: "We're trying to figure out who made these."

"Ah, the animal watches. This one was commissioned by a Mr Jacoby Dread," he said, pointing to Henry's. "It took me nearly two weeks to perfect all the details." He leaned in close to see Lang's. "But the wolf watch is not my work. Curious you should ask about these, just the other day a girl came in to inquire about these types of watches."

Henry and Lang looked at each other.

"Is this some kind of club or something? The 'Animal Pocket Watch Club?' Oh, I would love to join!"

"Yeah, it's a club," Henry said. "We're in the, uh... the..."

"Wolf and Crow Club," Lang finished with raised eyebrows.

"Right, the Wolf and Crow Club. Of course," said Henry "So this girl, did she want you to make a watch? Or did she already have one?"

"She already had one. It was brass with a spider. The work was a bit shoddy, I noticed the brass was dented and dull. Not nearly as fine as my work, and the time wasn't perfectly set, it was off by 1.57 seconds, and-"

"Mr Grigory?" Henry said, "Do you remember the girl's name? We might know her."

"Ah, her name. It was a funny one, so it was easy to remember. Persimmon Parsnip."

Henry shrugged. "Don't know her."

"She did leave her number, though. Said to give her a call in case someone else asked about an animal watch. Would you like it?"

Henry nodded. "Yes, that would be helpful."

Grigory searched through the many clocks around his neck, popping open the face of one with an intricate flower design. Inside was a paper slip with a phone number, which he copied for the boys. "Maybe I'll start a frog watch club. I just love frogs."

"Great idea. Thanks for the number."

"Any time. You boys have a Chim Chime day!"

Back outside they went in search of a payphone.

"Weird guy," Lang said.

"At least he seemed happy."

"There's a phone over there," said Lang pointing across the street. They put in some change, and Henry dialed the number Grigory had given him. Lang stuck his head close to the receiver so he could hear. After two rings, a woman's voice answered.

"Hello?"

"Hi, is this Persimmon Parsnip?" Henry said.

"This is her mother, Clementine. To whom am I speaking?"

"Henry Bats. May I speak with her?" He said, trying to sound polite.

"What is the matter of your call?"

"Uh, homework question."

There was a pause. "I suppose you may. One moment."

He heard a shuffle.

"Persimmon, it's for you. A boy named Henry Bats has a homework question."

There was a click and then the voice of a younger lady. "Homework question, huh? If this is that guy trying to sell Walpog repellent, I'm hanging up."

"It's not, please don't."

"What's this about then, Mr Henry Bats? How old are you, twelve?"

"Thirteen. My friend Lang and I just paid a visit to Grigory Chim. He told us you'd been there earlier."

The girl's tone changed, her voice lowered. "That's right."

"And he told us you asked about a pocket watch. We have them too."

There was a pause. "You mean *the* pocket watches?"

"Yes, *the* pocket watches."

"So that thing came to you for help?"

"Yes. Do you know what that thing was?"

"It said it was just a spirit looking for something important. Next thing I know this thing was around my neck and I have to tell everyone it's a fashion statement. I went to Chim Chime because I thought someone there made it."

"So you don't know?"

"Don't know what?"

Henry signed. "Maybe we should meet in person."

"Do you know how to get it off?"

"We think so."

"Hm. Okay, let's meet at The Shady Phantom. Know where that is?"

"I know," Lang said.

"We know where it is," Henry repeated.

"How about in half an hour? I think I could sneak out by then."

"It's a plan. See you soon, Persimmon."

"Ew, just call me Persi." She hung up the phone.

Chapter 6

Persimmon Parsnip Doesn't Care

"The Shady Phantom is near my house, I've passed it a few times," Lang said. "We'll have to take the bus back again."

They boarded the GrimBus and sat at the back where it was extra bumpy. Henry gazed out of the window at a dentist shop and turned to Lang. "Hey, if everything works out, which it will, what do you want to do?"

"What do you mean?"

"Like after we finish school. Do you want to be a dentist, or a chef, or an apprentice at Chim Chime, or what?"

Lang sat back into the dusty bus seat, thinking. "To be honest, I haven't really thought about it much, considering the circumstances. But I like science."

"Really?"

"Yeah. What about you?"

"For a while, I wanted to be a comic book illustrator, but as I've been informed by Hattie, I can't draw. But in Ms Squid's class I decided that if I can't illustrate comics, and we can't get these watches off, I'll collect them. That way when I die, I'll die a legend."

"As the owner of the largest comic book collection in history?"

"Yep."

"And how are you going to afford that?"

"I guess I'll have to work full time at Frank's Peculiar Pets. But then again, maybe I don't want to spend my last years working."

"At least they won't be spent in school." Lang smiled a bit, but Henry frowned.

"Are you scared of dying?"

Lang shrugged. "What bothers me most is what will happen to my dad when I'm gone."

"*If* you're gone," Henry said. "Don't give up yet."

"I'm not."

They exited the bus and Lang led the way to the Shady Phantom. It turned out to be a club beneath a real estate office. Inside, they were met with people dancing to ear-pounding music, throwing darts, and playing pool. They pushed their way to the tables, blinded by flashing green lights, and searched for a girl with a pocket watch around her neck. Over the thumping music, Henry heard someone yell his name. They turned to the direction of the voice, and there sitting at a table was Persimmon Parsnip. She looked to be fifteen, with a mass of red and purple streaked hair, ears covered in piercings, and clad in a corduroy jacket and ripped jeans. Around her neck was the spider watch. They sat down in chairs across from her.

"I could tell it was you because you looked so awkward wandering around," she yelled over the music. "I'm Persi. Henry, right? And what was your friend's name?"

"Lang," Henry shouted back.

Persi reached over and examined their watches with her orange lined, round eyes. "A wolf and a crow. Cool. So what is it I don't know about? And how do I get this thing off?"

"First of all, do you know what a Vytiper is?" Lang asked.

"Nope. Wait, is that a band?"

"No. Remember that shadowy thing that asked you for help?"

"Yeah, said it needed me to find something. It had me dig out this watch right next to a grave that said 'live fast, die young.'"

Lang leaned forward. "Do you mind if I take a closer look at it?"

"Yeah, go ahead."

They both leaned over to study the spider watch and discovered that only the 4th hour remained. "What a Vytiper does," Lang continued, "is shorten your life and use it for themselves so they can become human again, for a limited amount of time. According to your watch, you have about twenty years left to live."

Persi tilted her head to the side and scrunched her eyebrows. "You serious?"

"Dead serious."

"Twenty years…" she trailed off, the flashing lights reflecting in her eyes. With a deep thought, she slowly nodded her head. "That's plenty of time."

"What?" Henry said.

"That's enough time to see Twisted Hemlock in concert, go dark diving, buy a cycle, dye my hair every shade and then some."

"You mean you don't mind dying early?"

"Twenty years is an eternity."

"What about getting even? What about revenge?"

"Don't care. How much time do you guys have?"

"I have ten years. Lang has…"

"No years," he finished.

"That's really too bad. Let me know if I can help. And if you figure out how to get this stupid thing off my neck, give me a call."

Henry thumped his hand on the table. "So that's it?"

"Yeah, unless you want to stay and dance."

"No, I mean you're just accepting that you'll die early?"

"Pretty much. I was going to die someday anyway, right?"

"Fine. I guess we'll go then. Here." He wrote his number on paper from his backpack. "If you change your mind, give me a call."

"You got it."

They left The Shady Phantom, Henry in a huff. "How could she not care at all?"

"It's her decision," Lang said. "There's nothing we can do."

"But why is she just give up like that?"

"Maybe dying isn't the worst thing in the world. Let's just leave her alone, she might change her mind. Besides, we have other matters to attend to."

"Like the GrimMan?"

"Yep. We can go tonight."

"Into the forest."

"Mhm."

They looked beyond the crowded Grimworld buildings to the Penumbra Region edge where the dark, thick trees of the forest began.

"Remember all those stories about kids who went into the forest and never came out?" Henry said.

"Just a scare tactic by parents," Lang responded.

"Well I thought the GrimMan was a scare tactic too, but apparently he's real."

The two were in Lang's house, gathering things into their backpacks and eating leftover macaroni and cheese found in the refrigerator. Henry called Mildred to let her know he was staying the night at Lang's. She was delighted and mentioned that Hattie was staying at her new friend, Tabitha's house, which Henry thought was probably a lie.

"What if we get lost?" he said, shoving a forkful of macaroni into his mouth.

Lang searched around his desk and held up a compass. "This should do it. Okay, we have rope, paper, pencils, an umbrella, a first aid kit, and a flashlight. What else?"

"Snacks?"

Lang rolled his eyes. "I think that's the least of our worries."

"But just in case."

Lang complied and packed a bag of Sugar Slugs and two water bottles. "That's all I can think of."

"Are you going to leave your dad a note?"

"No, he won't be home until later. Hopefully, this won't take long."

Henry finished off his macaroni and slung on his backpack.

"I guess that means we're ready."

Lang put on his and nodded. "Ready."

They left the apartment and headed for the division between the forest and the Penumbra Region. In this case, the division was the abrupt end of an alleyway and the start of a tree wall. Any light that the gray sky provided was completely blocked out by the dense leaves and foliage. Lang took out the compass, got their bearings, and switched on the flashlight. For a split second they saw small, black masses dart from the light and out of sight. Henry gulped and took a few steps forward, officially crossing the border that meant they were now in the forest.

Chapter 7

The GrimMan Comes

"If that childhood rhyme is true, then we need to 'walk through the forest, dark and deep.' How far is dark and what makes it deep?" Henry said.

"Let's just walk for a few minutes. Then we'll try calling the GrimMan."

"If this doesn't work, I'm going to feel really stupid. I mean if we're going into the forest for noth-"

"Shh." Lang flicked the flashlight over to a large, contorted tree.

"What is it?" Henry whispered.

"Thought I heard something."

They stood still, watching the tree, but were only met with silence. As they began to move along, however, they heard rustles and snaps. Chills ran up and down Henry's spine like dozens of little spiders and his hair stood on end. The smell of moss and soil permeated the air. A Botsworth Tram rumbled in the distance on its way to the Umbra Region. Moments later they heard faint voices echo from the forest depths.

Lang swept the flashlight back and forth. "Can you believe someone had to build trams through here?"

"Well, we had to get to the other regions somehow."

"I heard lots of workers quit every day."

"I would have," Henry said. "How much further?"

"Just a bit, for good measure."

They crept past mushrooms that glowed green and yellow and puzzled their way through a knit of brambles and weeds. Henry found himself clenching his fists and hiking up his shoulders. He had the distinct feeling that at any second, something could reach out and grab him. They reached a small clearing and stopped.

"This is good," Lang said. "We can see better here."

"If the GrimMan really does come, what do we say?"

"We'll just explain the situation and see if he can help."

"And hope he doesn't eat us."

"Right. Let's call him together."

The two cleared their throats and chanted, "GrimMan, GrimMan, GrimMan." Henry strained his ears for music, but the forest was silent.

"Let's try again," Lang said.

They spoke the name louder this time. Henry's ears perked at a soft, faraway music box chime. The sound seemed to come from all directions, and Lang spun around with the light.

"I'm regretting this decision," Henry said.

The eerie tune grew louder until the music source was only inches away. In Lang's flashlight beam, a figure emerged from the forest. Sitting inside a wooden cart was a man turning a music box crank. He wore a striped suit and a top hat sat above his long, gray face. The flesh from his forehead extends out into a thin rod that curved downwards ending in a glowing yellow bulb that bobbed in front of his face. His lower body was squished inside the cart, his round torso spilling out the sides, his proportions big and distorted, human, yet not human. The large black music box sat on his stomach, the lid open to reveal the pin drum playing the off-key, haunting tune as he turned the crank.

Henry forced himself to look at the GrimMan's face, illuminated by the sickly yellow bobbing light. What should have been the whites of his eyes were black pits, the pupils gangrenous yellow, and he bore a grin that stretched from ear to ear revealing a set of long, needle-like teeth. Henry's breath grew shallow.

The wheels of the cart turning and creaking as the GrimMan came closer.

Lang's hand shook holding the flashlight, but they otherwise stood frozen.

With his broad smile and unblinking eyes, the GrimMan spoke in a deep, garbled voice that, just like the music, surrounded them from all directions.

"Someone called the GrimMan?"

Henry could barely force out the word, "Yes." The GrimMan flicked in and out of focus like a bad television signal and disappeared.

"Problems of children." The voice came from behind them. They whipped around and the GrimMan's face loomed only inches from theirs, his body leaning from the cart. "What is your problem?" Henry stumbled backwards and the GrimMan's smile got impossibly wider as he eyed their necks. "Pocket watches?"

Lang spoke with stilted words. "Yes, from Vytipers. We read there was a reversal."

The GrimMan nodded his head once. "One came before."

"Who?" Henry asked.

"Ezekiel Dread."

"Dread? Was he a Vytiper?"

"No. Wanted a reversal. Brother Zachary Dread was first Vytiper." His eyes flashed. "You want reversal."

"Yes," Lang said.

The GrimMan circled around them in his cart, the wheels lurching as they bumped over the debris on the forest floor, and he spoke in rhythm with his music box tune.

"Hair from the Vytiper, blood of the reaped, one part worm, a Botsworth Bar, steeped.

A piece of Red Beryl and a sprig of Boosprit, a Spotted Harvestman and Zap Sap, just a bit.

Brew in a pot and fill the chamber. With a hand from the Vytiper, they'll meet their maker.

Set back time to 12 o'clock, and only then shall the watches fall off."

He quickly turned the music box crank and a piece of withered paper rolled out from the pin drum. With his other hand, he held out the paper but pulled back when Henry tried to take it. "First something for me."

"What?" Lang said.

The GrimMan clicked his teeth. "Hungry."

Henry's heart pumped in his ears. "You're hungry?"

"Botsworth Bar. I want another."

"We don't have any," Henry said.

The GrimMan tilted his head so it was parallel with the ground "No Botsworth Bar?"

"No."

"Stomach is empty." The GrimMan quivered and disappeared. Henry and Lang spun around, but he was nowhere to be seen.

"Did he leave?" Henry asked, squinting into the darkness.

"I don't think so, the music's still here."

They heard a click above them and looked up. The GrimMan, cart and all, was hovering above the boys upside down. His mouth was open and stretched like a snake ready to swallow a rat.

"Wait!" Henry shouted. "We have something else." He ripped open Lang's backpack and with a trembling hand held up the Sugar Slug bag. "Delicious cereal."

The GrimMan relaxed his open jaws. "Cereal?"

"It's got sugar in it, just like a Botsworth Bar."

In half a second the GrimMan flashed from above them to right-side-up on the ground. He took the bag from Henry, put the whole thing in his mouth, and swallowed. His eyes nearly popped out of his head.

"Good. Full now." He handed the paper to Henry. "Another calls my name."

The GrimMan wavered in and out of focus for the last time and vanished. The music box tune ceased, and the boys were left with the heavy forest silence.

Henry heaved a sigh and tried to loosen his tense muscles.

"We just met the GrimMan."

"Yep," Lang said, flashlight still shaking in his hand.

"We can undo this now." Henry carefully folded the paper, which contained the rhyme and tucked it inside his backpack. "Let's get out of here."

Lang pulled out the compass and a frown spread across his face. He tapped the compass with his index finger and shook it back and forth. "It's not working."

"Seriously?" Henry saw that the needle was swiveling around wildly. "It's one thing after another."

"Just stay calm." He looked around, squinting through the dim light, then pointed at a tree branch that grew at an odd angle from its trunk. "I think that tree looks familiar."

They moved cautiously on legs that quivered like jelly, still shaken from the encounter.

"So Zachary Dread was the first Vytiper," Lang said.

"Guess it runs in the family. And Ezekiel was looking for a reversal. Do you think Zachary used Ezekiel to become a Vytiper?"

"That would be my guess. Though whether or not he was able to undo it, we don't know."

"Jacoby would know."

"Let's hope we don't get the chance to ask anytime soon."

Henry nodded. "By the way, I think you've learned an important lesson from me."

"What's that?"

"Always bring snacks."

Lang grinned. "Guess you're right. Do you really think he was going to eat us?"

"I think so." Henry shivered. "I don't know how I'm going to sleep tonight."

"Well, we won't be sleeping in the forest, considering I can see a light ahead."

They ran ahead, mindless of the thick brambles that snatched at their legs. As they drew nearer they could see the light was an ectolantern mounted on a fencepost, softly lighting a small park with a slide and swings.

"We made it," Henry said.

"And we're not too far from my house."

Back at Lang's apartment, Henry climbed on top of the bunkbed and collapsed. "This has been the longest day of my life." He counted on his fingers, "First the library, then your house, then Chim Chime, then the Shady Phantom, then back to your house, then the forest of all places, and finally back here again."

"I think we'll sleep alright after all," Lang said, nearly asleep on the bottom bunk.

"And there's still so much more to do. A whole poem of things. I mean, where should we start? Lang?..." Henry peeked over the side and found him fast asleep. He plopped his head back on the pillow and closed his eyes.

Chapter 8

Hattie Reveals Her Hobby

Henry woke up with his leg and arm dangling over the side of the bunk bed. Lang tapped his foot from beneath.

"You up?"

"Yeah," Henry said. "I'm hungry."

They arose and went in search of breakfast. In the kitchen they instead found Lang's father sitting at the table reading the *Daily Gray*. He peered over his paper and seemed startled to see Henry. Henry thought he looked like an older, taller version of Lang with his short black hair and calm eyes.

"Dad, this is Henry Bats," Lang said. "Remember I told you about him?"

He jumped up and shook Henry's hand. "That's right, the boy you've been spending time with. Nice to meet you, I'm Barnaby."

"Nice to meet you, too."

"You had a sleepover, Langley?" Barnaby said, smiling.

Lang nodded and his dad went to the fridge and rummaged through its contents. "Glad to have you over, Henry. You boys are probably hungry. We don't have much, but I think I have a few eggs in here. Scratch that, they're expired. There's macaroni, but... hey, where'd the macaroni go?"

"It's okay Dad, we're heading out soon anyway."

"Are you sure? Well, here." He gave Lang money from his wallet. "You two have a nice breakfast out in the Penumbra today."

"Thanks, Dad."

He nodded. "I hope to see you again, Henry."

"Thanks, Mr Skullfield."

They made their way to RIP, upon Henry's suggestion. "Your

dad seems nice," he said.

"He is."

They were seated in a rigatoni booth and after they had given their order, Henry pulled out the poem the GrimMan had given them.

"Okay, let's go through this line by line. Hair from the Vytiper, the blood of the reaped. Getting our blood is easy, but this means we'll have to find Greta Flingbossom and see Jacoby again. Next is two parts worm and a Botsworth Bar."

"A Botsworth Bar should be easy, but aren't worms in the forest? I'd rather not go in there again."

Henry thought of the worm lady. "I know an alternative."

"That pet shop you work at?"

"No, Frank uses crickets and flies. But the rhyme says we need a Spotted Harvestman, he might have those. It's a kind of spider."

"Next is Red Beryl and Boosprit."

Farfallo the waiter came and set down stroganoff for Lang and pesto for Henry. "Enjoy, you two."

From the top of his dish, Henry plucked off a purple sprig with three holes in each leaf that looked like tiny frowning faces. "Your wish is my command."

"Is that Boosprit?"

"Sure is."

Lang shook his head. "How many times have you eaten here to know the pesto comes with that?"

"Too many to count, but I bet you're glad I have."

"You must be made of pasta. Well, that's one down. What about the Red Beryl and Zap Sap?"

"Not sure, but they have to be somewhere."

"Okay, let's split up. You find out about the Harvestman and I'll see about the red beryl. Meet after school tomorrow?"

"Yep."

They finished eating and Henry left for Frank's Peculiar Pets.

A sharp hiss greeted his ears as he stepped into the store. Frank looked up from the unruly hissing cockroach he was tending. "Henry, got time to mist some lizards?"

Henry got to work spritzing Dustyskin Geckos. "Hey Frank, do you happen to have any Spotted Harvestmen on order?"

"I've got some striped coming in, but spotted are hard to come by, you know." He shook his hand. "Darn thing bit me."

"Why are they hard to come by?"

"The breeder I know is all the way in the Antumbra Region. Otherwise only place you can get 'em are the mines, and you have to go down deep."

"As in the mines under Grimworld?"

"No, the ones in your nose."

"Very funny. But how do you get in?"

"Looking for a little adventure, are we?" Frank secured the cockroach in a cage.

"I read about the Harvestman in a book, just thought it looked cool."

"Well, the old entrances are blocked off and I doubt they'd let you in at the current site. Sorry kid, I don't think you'll see a Spotted Harvestman anytime soon."

Henry bit his lip to hide his disappointment. "Oh well."

But when he got home in time for lunch, all Henry could think about was getting into the mines. Time was of the essence. Everyone sat around the table eating overly toasted sandwiches. The Thread-Spinner strings that crisscrossed the table were drying and shrinking from the spray his parents had bought. Once Mildred ran out of questions about his stay at Lang's, Henry brought up the topic.

"Is there a way to tour the mines?"

Hattie stopped mid-bite.

"The mines?" Gobbert said. "Why?"

Grandpa Flemm jerked in his chair. "Did you say rind? *Lettuce* rinds?"

"No Grandpa, *mines.* I was just wondering."

"I don't think they offer tours, do they Gobbert?" Said Mildred.

"I don't think so."

"What about ones they've abandoned?"

"Those are all closed off, Hen, they're dangerous."

"Why would you want to get into them?" Mildred asked.

"Well Frank was talking about these really cool spiders, but you can only get them from underground."

Gobbert glanced at Mildred. "You stay out of the mines now, Henry."

"I will."

Finishing his sandwich, he went off to tend to Corn Chip in his room.

"Why do you want to get into the mines?"

He turned around. Hattie stepped inside, closed the door, and folded her arms. "Does this have to do with that code from yesterday? And that watch you're always wearing? The writing I translated mentions a watchmaker."

"Why does it matter to you, I thought we had a deal?"

"Because I want to get into the mines, too."

Henry stared at her. "Huh?"

"If you tell me why you're going, then I'll tell you why I am."

He scratched his head. "It's...well...you go first."

"Fine, but you have to pinky swear you'll tell me."

He did so and sat on the bed, Hattie in his desk chair.

"That time you saw me with a group of people, well, it's a kind of club. The Uncanny Club."

"You run around in the streets?"

"No. We explore."

"Explore what?"

"Grimworld. Or the Penumbra Region, to be exact. We've been to Dire Ghost Town, Clotty Cave, Grisly's Passage, and now we want to get into the mines. And I think we're close to finding a way."

"So that's what you've been up to. Mom and Dad would flip if they found out. You went to Clotty Cave?"

"They're not going to find out. And yes, the rumors are true. There is a Whispering Banshee. Your turn."

Henry cleared his throat. "Okay. Well. You were right about the code and the watch being part of it."

She nodded. "I knew it."

"Basically, I can't get the watch off until I finish a few tasks, and one of them is getting a Spotted Harvestman from the mines."

"Why can't you get the watch off?"

"So, remember that Nightspook that moved your dolls?"

"Yeah."

"Did it ever talk to you, or look like a shadowy thing?"

"Nightspooks can't do that."

"That's what I thought until it showed up in my room and asked for help. See, it wasn't a Nightspook." Hattie tilted her head. "It was a thing called a Vytiper. Actually, it used to be human. Well, it still is, kind of."

She raised her eyebrows and twirled a strand of her blonde hair between her fingers. "You expect me to believe this?"

"No, really. The night it disappeared was when it tricked me into finding this watch. Next thing I know, it's stuck around my neck." He patted the watch under his shirt and explained meeting Lang, finding Jacoby Dread, infiltrating his mansion, decoding the book, and meeting the GrimMan. He showed her the decoded notes and the poem from the GrimMan as proof.

"But why do you need to get the watch off so badly?"

He sighed. "Because when the watch hand gets to the number 2, I'll die. It'll happen in about 10 years."

Hattie frowned. "You'll die?"

"Yeah. Lang's watch is almost there. He doesn't have much time left."

She stood up and paced the room. "You're telling me this Jacoby Dread guy took your life for himself?"

"Yes."

"And you swear you're telling the truth?" Hattie eyed him square in the face.

"I promise."

"If you're lying, you're dead." She sat back in the desk chair and folded her arms. "Only ten years?"

"Yeah. Hattie, I need to get into the mines. I have time to figure this out, but Lang doesn't. And it's not just us, either. His brother died from a Vytiper, and there's this girl, Persi."

Hattie stood up. "We'll get your watches off, okay? I'll help. I'm not going to let my brother die, and I'm not going to let Lang die, either."

"Thank you, Hattie." Henry breathed a sigh of relief. "It's been hard hiding this from you and Mom and Dad."

"Why didn't you tell them?"

"Didn't want them to worry." She nodded and headed for the door. "Where are you going?"

"I have some research to do. Thanks for telling me." With that, she left his room.

Mildred stopped Henry after school while she stirred a pot of something that smelled like radishes, but not quite.

"Hen, someone called for you. She said her name was Persi."

"Really? Thanks, Mom."

She watched him, waiting. When he was about to go to his room she said, "So, who's this Persi?"

"Just someone I know. And before you ask anything else, she's old. Like three years older than me."

Her eyes lit up. "Another friend? I'm so happy for you, Hen."

"Mom. Stop."

After dinner, while everyone was watching television, he made the call to Persi from the kitchen.

"Parsnip Palace, who's this?" came Persi's voice.

He whispered into the phone, "Hi Persi, this is Henry Bats. My mom said you called?"

"Yeah, so about all this Vytiper business, I was doing some calculations and if I only have twenty years left to live, it looks like I won't be able to fit in Bot Gliding, shark feeding, and Walpog-catching."

"Ok. Sorry to hear that."

"So I'm in. Whatever you need me to do to get this watch off, I'll do it."

Henry grinned. "I was hoping you'd come around."

"Yeah, well, there's a lot I need to get done this lifetime."

"Good. Lang and I found a list of things we'll need to get, and there's a few we'll have trouble with, like whatever Red Beryl is, hair from the Vytiper, Zap Sap-"

"Zap Sap. I'm on it."

"You can get that?"

"My mom works at a plant nursery, it's no problem."

"Okay. That's great. Give me a call when you get it."

"Will do."

"Otherwise, you need to find your Vytiper and get their hair. You said you went to an unmarked grave?"

"Yes, but I have a few clues as to who it might be."

"Alright, keep me posted."

He hung up the phone and his eyes strayed to a black box trapped behind a spice bottle wall. "Hm." He pulled it out and inspected the nametag, which read 'To Henry Bats.' He held it up in the living room. "What's this?" He asked everyone.

"Lettuce?" Flemm leaned forward from the couch.

"Oh, I forgot someone left that by the door. You're quite the popular boy today," Mildred said. "That's not from this Persi, is it?"

"Who's Persi?" Hattie's ears practically twitched.

"No one," he said, and fled to his room. Brow furrowed, he

pulled the twine string that was wrapped around the box and lifted the lid. Inside was a money stack and a note. It read:

Dear Henry Bats,

I do think it would be in your best interest to bring back my book. Yours truly, Jacoby Dread.

P.S. I hope you will put this to better use than tossing it in my fountain.

Henry's heart skipped a beat.

Chapter 9

Morton Crawly Brings Stickers

"I told Hattie about the watches."

"What? Why?" Lang said.

The two were walking home from school.

"As it turns out, she's trying to get into the mines, too. She's part of some weird exploration thing called the Uncanny Club."

"So she knows a way in?"

"She's working on it. Also, Persi called. She's in too, she's getting Zap Sap."

"Really?"

"Yep. And Jacoby Dread sent me a package with money and a note saying to bring back the book."

"Whoa, really?

"I guess he finally figured out we took it. So what should we do? Give it back?"

"This is a lot of new information in the span of a minute." Lang scratched his head. "Ok, let's see. We don't need the book anymore. As long as we keep the translated papers, we should be fine."

"Want to head over now?"

"Actually do you think you could do it? My dad's driving the bus today, he wants to take me for a ride. Here, I've been keeping it with me." He pulled out the book from his backpack.

"If I'm not in school tomorrow, you're in charge of my search party. I feel like he's going to put me in a secret dungeon or something."

"You'll be alright. Just don't let him catch on that we know what the book says. And try to get one of his hairs."

Henry made his way to Sable Avenue. A light drizzle materialized from the gloomy sky and collected on his eyelashes.

This time the Dread Manor gates were attended by two guards, large men dressed in gray overcoats.

"I'm Henry Bats," he said, staring up at the men.

They looked at each other, nodded, and opened the gate. Henry walked through and casually tossed the money bundle Jacoby had given him into the cherub fountain. The front door was opened by his old friend Ferdinand, eyes as lifeless as ever. "Right this way," he said.

Ferdinand led Henry to the right wing of the mansion, past the knights and contorted animal statues that twisted around like clay, into a room plastered with dingy yellow curtains contrasting the gray brick walls. A candle chandelier hung in the center over a dining table with two chairs, one of which was occupied by Jacoby Dread. He was reading a newspaper, sipping tea. In front of him was a bite-sized dessert assortment perfectly centered on a black tray.

"Mr Henry Bats," Ferdinand announced and stationed himself beside the wall.

Jacoby turned a newspaper page. "Have a seat. Feel free to eat as many Screampuffs as you want." Henry sat down and put the book on his lap. "The groundskeeper found your reward money in the fountain. What a waste, it's all wrinkly now," he said, his eyes glued to the paper. "I see you brought the book."

"If this is all you want, can I just give it to you and go?"

"I have some questions. First, how did you find out about it? I assume that's why you were trailing water around the dining hall at midnight."

He answered honestly, "We didn't know about the book beforehand, we just thought you were hiding something. We found grayprints in your office."

"I see. And I'm sure you've noticed the book is written in code."

"We did."

"Have you figured out what it says?"

"No. We even tried to figure it out at Botsworth Library."

Jacoby glanced at him over the newspaper. "Tell me then, why are you giving it back so readily? Don't you want to know what it says after all your effort?"

Henry dropped the book in front of him and slid it across the table. "I want you to tell me yourself. There's no way we're cracking this thing." What Henry really wanted to ask about was Zachary and Ezekiel Dread, but he held his tongue.

"What if I don't tell you?" Jacoby raised his eyebrows, slightly amused.

"You should be asking what happens if you do."

His interest piqued, he put the newspaper down and interlaced his fingers. "Tell me, what do I get?"

Henry crossed his arms and sat back in the chair. "Hattie and her dolls will come over for a tea party."

Jacoby tilted his head and twiddled his mustache in thought with his one gloved hand. "How many dolls?"

"All of them."

"This is something she would like to do?"

"I already asked and she's looking forward to it. You wouldn't want to disappoint her, would you?"

Jacoby slowly shook his head. "I'll give you the basics of what the book says. Deal?"

"Deal."

"Essentially, Vytipers are immortal beings, whether in shadow form or human form. It gives a list of means by which one can become a Vytiper and a bit more on the properties of being so. That's it."

"Why didn't you want me to find out?" Henry said.

"Because I don't want it available to the public. This was supposed to be a family secret and it's already been leaked. Are you satisfied with that answer?"

Henry pretended to think about it. "I am."

"Good. No more excursions into the Manor?"

"Doubtful."

"Now then, when will this tea party be? I can arrange my schedule at any time."

"Probably on a weekend. I'll let you know."

"Very well. Tell Hattie I look forward to seeing her. You may leave."

With nothing else to say and no chance of getting Jacoby's hair without raising suspicion, Henry left.

The next day Henry walked with Lang after school, intending for him to meet the new Stink Toad at Frank's, and updating him on his visit to the manor.

"You think Jacoby believed we didn't translate it?" Lang said.

"Yeah, I think he thinks we're dumb. Also, in return for wanting to know what was in the book, I offered Jacoby a doll tea party with Hattie."

Lang nearly choked. "Let me get this straight. A tea party is something he wanted to do, not Hattie?"

"Yep."

"What about me?"

They both turned around to find Hattie behind them. She was wearing a long black dress with heavy boots and her school backpack was stuffed full.

"Where did you come from?" Henry said.

"Side alleyway." She looked at Lang. "I'm sorry to hear about the watches."

"It's alright. We're getting closer to a solution," Lang said.

"What do you want, Hattie?"

Her mouth twisted into a grin. "I know how to get into the mines."

"Really?" Both boys chimed.

"Morton Crawly, the Uncanny Club leader, his dad works at Botsworth Fun Park. There have been rumors of a closed-off mine there. Well, Morton found it, and we're going to conduct a special mission with you. The sooner the better." They nodded. "Then let's go."

Botsworth Fun Park was squished into the middle of the Penumbra Region, a twenty-minute walk from school. It was so squished, that some of the roller coasters whizzed past the windows of neighboring apartment buildings, and water from splash rides startled tenants when they came home from work. Someone dressed up as a jolly Botsworth Bar danced to the carnival music and greeted the trio as they arrived. Henry and Lang started for the ticket line, but Hattie caught them by the sleeve.

"Over there." She pointed to a boy wearing a baggy sweatshirt, a baseball cap, and an oversized backpack by the fence that blocked off the park.

He waved them over and put his finger to his lips. "Shh." The boy scanned the area and waited until the ticket attendants only a few feet away were all busy, and the park security guard had turned his back. He pushed a fence section and flipped it up. They scurried underneath and emerged behind the Soul Sweeper Rollercoaster. The boy reset the fence section and held out his hand. "Morton Crawly."

"Henry Bats," said Henry, shaking Morton's hand.

"Langley Skullfield."

Morton looked at them with dark eyes framed by extra bushy eyebrows. "Heard you wanted to get into the mines."

"Hattie said you had a way," Henry said.

"I have a way. Follow my lead." He weaved through the crowd of children with their reluctant parents. "So what do you need a Harvestman for?"

"For now, that's strictly confidential," Lang said.

Morton nodded. "One of those things."

"Why do you need to get into the mines?"

"As the leader of the Uncanny Club, it's my duty to explore the unexplored."

The smell of Coffin Candy and hot dogs mingled in the air and a flurry of screams came from the Maniacal Teacups ride. Morton stopped at a sign that announced 'Sunken River.' "We'll need to get on this ride." They waited in line and piled into a small boat that floated on green, sludgy water. They drifted slowly, painfully, into a tunnel filled with animatronic fish bending to and fro. A few metal eels squirmed above them and rusty piranhas rose from the water with the speed of a snail. The boat continued to drift along, winding through the tunnel, the sounds of the park fading away.

"I forgot how boring this ride was," Henry said.

Morton stood up on the boat. "Well, it's about to get a whole lot more interesting. Here's our stop." He stretched his leg to the tunnel edge and hopped onto a ledge where a crocodile was snapping its toothless jaw. Henry followed and could now see the outline of a door concealed with paint to match the tunnel. Morton pulled a key out of his pocket and unlocked it. "I fished the river with a net for weeks until I found this."

He pushed the door open, and before them was pitch black darkness.

"Flashlights," Morton said. "I have extras for Henry and Lang."

They all shone their flashlights into the darkness to reveal the old mine held up by wood beams and laden with cart tracks. They took a few steps in and the door shut behind them, the grating animatronic sound disappearing from Henry's ears.

"Alright, our mission is to get a Spotted Harvestman," Hattie said.

"And to not get lost," Morton added. From his other pocket, he took out a Steel Chancellor sticker pack. "We'll put these on the tunnel walls."

"Steel Chancellor, cool. Are these the new ones?" Henry asked.

Hattie rolled her eyes. "Now's not the time for comic book

talk."

They began to walk along the wooden tracks, going deeper and deeper into Grimworld. A few cave spiders scurried beneath their feet, Henry keeping his eye out for a Harvestman. "Why did they abandon this place, anyway?" He said.

Morton turned to look at him. "According to our research, someone made some miscalculations and started mining under the forest. I guess things got a bit hairy and it really spooked the workers. They couldn't find anyone to work down here so they abandoned this network. Turned it into an amusement park instead."

"This mine is actually one of the oldest," Hattie chimed in. "It's supposed to go down for miles."

When they came to a split in the tunnel, Morton stopped and put a sticker on the wall. "Right or left?"

"Right," Lang said. "If we always go right, getting out shouldn't be too hard."

A few water drops plonked onto Henry's face from above them. The mine walls had changed from packed dirt when they first entered, to a rugged stone. "Most buildings are made up of this, huh?" Henry said.

Lang touched the rock. "Soulzite. This is what they were mining."

They continued on and Henry could feel a slight breeze on his face. It wasn't until a few minutes later that he realized something was off.

"Do you guys feel that?"

"Feel what?" Morton said.

Henry held his hand out in front of him. "It feels like wind."

"We're heading downwards, deeper into the mines, right?"

"That's right," said Lang.

"So why is there wind?"

They all stopped in their tracks. Lang furrowed his eyebrow. "Hopefully it's just a natural phenomenon."

"Wait a minute," Hattie said. "I think I remember reading about this in my research. After they started mining under the forest, a wind started blowing through the mine shafts."

"So it's not some monster breathing or something?" Henry said.

"I don't think so."

"We keep going then." Morton continued to lead the way.

"Are you looking for anything in particular down here?" Henry asked.

"Nope. Just exploring and logging our findings. Hattie will write an official report in the Uncanny Book when we get back."

"So what were you guys up to when I came out of that tavern?" Henry asked.

"Oh, that was my first report," Hattie said. "There's an abandoned mortuary on that street. You wouldn't believe the number of Death Pebbles."

They walked along the rusty mine tracks, passing leftover tools and carts filled with rubble. Henry shivered thinking about the people that had once worked here.

They took another right turn into a larger mine section, a spot where the Soulzite was abundant. While Morton put a Steel Chancellor sticker on a wood beam, Lang inspected the area. "Henry, over here," he said and pointed to a cart filled with ground Soulzite. Sitting on top was a spider the width of a thumb, its black body patched with red splotches. "Is this what we're looking for?"

Henry knew right away that it was the Spotted Harvestman. "That's it." The leap of his heart at the discovery ended quickly. "I don't have a container to put it in."

Morton dropped his backpack to the floor and dug through it. "The Uncanny Club is always prepared." He pulled out a small plastic tub and handed it to Henry. "You'll have to get the spider though, I'm not a fan."

Henry opened the tub and cautiously set it on its side on the

Soulzite a few inches from the spider. He cupped his hand in order to guide the spider into the trap. From inside the pile of ground stone, hundreds of tiny Harvestmen emerged, disturbed by the movement. They were black with a single red spot, and several scurried up Henry's hand. Morton backed away to the mine wall, and Hattie and Lang watched in fascination.

"Good thing these aren't poisonous," Henry said, and simply scooped up a tub-full of Soulzite, catching at least six of the baby spiders. He shook his arm and they fell to the ground like eight-legged raindrops. "Mission accomplished." He stuck the tub in his backpack and looked at Morton. "Is there anything else you need to do down here?"

"I think we've explored this mine sufficiently, don't you think Hattie?"

"I'd say so."

"Then, mission accomplished." He headed for the stickered beam and stopped abruptly.

"What's wrong?" Hattie said.

A strong wind passed through the mine and nearly blew off Morton's hat. "The sticker switched beams. I definitely put it on this one, the passage we came through." He touched the left beam and stood silently.

"We've been taking every right passageway," Lang agreed.

"But how did it switch?" Morton said to himself. He shook his head. "It doesn't matter, just be sure to log this, Hattie. We'll go back through the passage we know we came from."

He strode ahead and the others followed, glancing over their shoulders as they went. Henry felt an uneasiness in the pit of his stomach. The passage they were on soon split into three directions, and the Steel Chancellor sticker directed them to the middle.

"What's going on?" Morton said, peeling the sticker off to examine it with his flashlight. "These should always be on the leftmost passage." He pushed forward to the left and again and again, the stickers were not where they should be, and soon, they came to a split where there were no stickers at all. "Stay right here," he said and sprinted back the way they had come.

"What's going on?" Henry said.

Hattie's face was pale. "I think I have an idea. I'm betting we're under the forest right now."

Morton appeared around the corner, panting, "Where we just came from there were two splits, now there's three. The mines are switching around."

"What should we do?" Henry said.

"We just have to keep going and hope for the best."

This was not the answer Henry wanted to hear. They continued, always choosing the leftmost passage until they reached a sign planted in a cart. It read: *Beware the Dirt Adalis.*

"Dirt Adalis?" Hattie tilted her head.

Lang shrugged. "Whatever it is, we probably shouldn't risk running into it."

All four of them turned around and in sync, a look of dread spread across their faces. The passage end was solidly closed off by planks and rocks. Morton spoke in a higher pitched voice. "Guess we're running into it."

The mine tracks they had consistently been on ended at an abrupt curve in the passage. When they rounded it, they emerged into a large, open cavern. It was a large pocket of space with long, tooth-like stalactites above them that dripped water into a small mineral pool. Surrounding the pool were abandoned buckets and picks, and even a few items of clothing. The water glowed a bright white that illuminated the cave walls and revealed gray Soulzite sheets. Only, on every surface of these enormous slabs of Soulzite were hundreds of large holes that tunneled into the rock. They were the size of a small car and covered the cavern from top to bottom. Looking at them sent chills up Henry's spine. "What are those?"

"They're not mining tunnels since there's some on the ceiling of the cave," Lang said.

Morton took a few steps forward. "Well, we've got to get to the other side, I think I see where the exit is. We'll have to go around the water."

The others cautiously followed, the wind creating a slight whistle as it swept through the cavern. They reached the pool edge and looked into the cloudy, rocky water. An old mining shirt lay nearby, its once green color faded to a dull gray. Henry thought the ground underneath his feet might be trembling ever so slightly but dismissed it as his imagination. They made it halfway around the pool, but a strange crunching noise stopped them. It came from above and sounded like rocks being rubbed together.

"What's that?" Hattie whispered.

She quickly got her answer. From in between two stalactite clumps, five long, brown tendrils violently stabbed through a solid slab of Soulzite. Shards of rock crashed down into the pool with a plonk. The sticky brown tendrils curled and uncurled and flicked to and fro as if studying their surroundings. More tendrils poked through the Soulzite, smaller bits of rock tumbling down with them. The tendrils attached themselves to the ceiling and through the hole oozed the worm-like body they were attached to. The creature was long and gelatinous looking. Its lively tendrils stuck out from its body at all angles like branches from a tree. The head ended in a point with no other features.

The Dirt Adalis dangled half its body from the hole it had created and waved back and forth in the breeze.

Chapter 10

The Night of Smokebrights

Henry stood, frozen, then glanced at the others. Hattie met his gaze and mouthed, "Dirt Adalis. What do we do?"

He pointed to the tunnel that exited the cave. They all took a step towards it. The rocky ground crunched beneath their feet and the Adalis' body became rigid and ceased its swaying. Morton grabbed Henry's sweatshirt to stop him from walking forward and zipped his fingers across his lips. They waited in silence while the Adalis kept completely still, listening for movement. When it heard nothing, it churned the rest of the way out from the hole it had made, its tendrils adhering to the rock as it slid down. It took no notice of the children standing beneath it, and Henry became sure it couldn't see.

It wound around the previous holes it had dug and made its way to the cave floor. Using its tendrils to inspect the ground, it came closer and closer to the group.

"Now what," Henry mouthed to Lang.

Lang slowly bent down and picked up a rock, the others catching on to his idea. The Adalis came close enough so they could see the lined pattern of its transparent skin. Sweat fell down Henry's forehead, and he had to grip his knees to keep his legs from shaking. Lang held his hand up and counted down on his fingers, three... two... one. He pelted the rock across the mineral pool and it landed on the other side with an echoing thunk. The Adalis raised its pointed head and its tendrils froze simultaneously for a moment. In the next second, its body scrunched together like a coiled spring and launched itself in a zigzag pattern across the water to where the rock had landed.

"Run," Lang whispered.

Henry kicked off the ground and hurdled over rocks and

mining tools. Blood pumped in his ears, the exit tunnel in sight. He glanced behind him to see Morton's terrified face and glimpsed the Adalis refocusing its attention from the rock to the scurry of people. His heart immediately sunk.

"It's coming," he said in what little breath he could muster.

"Everyone stop," Lang hissed.

They all slid to a halt, a cloud of ancient dust particles stirred up around them. The Adalis sped back across the water and wriggling its large body in the dust, its tendrils frantic with confusion, a few dangerously close to lashing Hattie. Without time to think, Henry sprinted sideways, directing the Adalis' attention towards him and yelled "Get out," to the others. The creature bobbed its head back and forth, focusing on the sound. It again coiled its body and its head flew forward like a projectile straight at Henry. He could see how the bottom half of its head peeled open to reveal a circle of pointed teeth stuck into its gummy mouth, tendrils streaming back with its speed. He jerked back at the last second, the creature's vicious strike missing him by inches.

Henry was now faced with the obstacle of the Adalis' body being between him and the cave exit. Already it was preparing for another attack as it swiveled around, trying to locate its target. Henry swooped his hand down and picked up a rock. With blind fear, he heaved it behind him and froze in place, waiting to see if the Adalis would take the bait. More rock sounds echoed through the cave and Henry turned his head ever so slightly to see his companions at the exit tunnel, throwing everything they could find in random directions. Confused, the Adalis swung its head around toward each sound but made no move. Henry quieted his breath as much as he could and stealthily moved around the beast. When he accidentally kicked a rock or crunched through a dirt pile, it turned in his direction but was soon distracted by the other sounds. Henry came closer and closer to the exit, his heart beating like a hammer. He reached the trio and Morton held up one last rock.

"Go," he whispered and threw it.

Henry sprinted through the tunnel, not daring to look back. They made it halfway to a curve, and he could only hope that the passageways would reorder themselves. He could hear the Adalis behind them, sliding across the dirt and rocks. It sounded as though it was about to lunge. But when they turned the corner, all was silent. They collapsed on the ground and Morten cautiously peeked back through the passage. "All...clear," he said with stilted breath.

Henry blotted the sweat from his face with his sleeve. "I hate worms."

"Why did you run to it like that?" Lang said, leaning against the wall.

Henry pulled out his pocket watch. "It's not my time to die yet."

"But we don't know that. We don't know if you can die before the watch says your time is up."

"Well, better I take a risk than you. You're getting close to running out, who knows if this is what would've killed you."

"What's all this about death and watches?" Morton said.

They both looked at him. "Tell you later." Henry heaved himself up from the ground. "First, let's make it out of here alive."

While they were talking, Hattie had wandered to the passage end. "I think we're back on track," she called. "There's a sticker on the left fork."

"Phew," Morton said. "Let's go."

To their great relief, the stickers continued on the left passages. Morton and Hattie marched on, while Henry and Lang trailed behind.

"You know, we don't even know *how* it ends," Henry said.

"What do you mean?"

"When time runs out, if we just drop dead or what."

"As opposed to being hit by a bus, or death by Dirt Adalis?"

"Yeah. The case files in Mutter's Grand List of Entities said they died from an unknown cause. Who knows what that could be? Maybe it would be safer if you stay in your house. Just in case."

"I don't think that'll do me any good. Besides, I've already accepted what's going to happen, Henry."

"It's not going to happen."

"But if it does. Just don't worry about me."

"Of course I'm going to worry about you." Henry stopped and grabbed Lang's watch. "Look, the minute hand is nearly on the one. We have to do everything we can to stop you from dying."

Lang looked at him firmly. "You don't get it. I'm doing this for you, Henry."

"What do you mean?"

"I'm going on this crazy hunt for you. So *you* can live."

Henry narrowed his eyes. "Why are you so set on dying? You can live too, Lang. We're figuring it out."

"All I'm saying is for me, it's not a big deal."

Henry stopped and grabbed Lang's shoulder. "It is a big deal."

"Guys, up here." Hattie's voice called from ahead. "It's the door."

Henry let go of Lang's shoulder. "We'll talk about this later."

The two caught up.

"We made it," Morton said.

They slipped out and closed the door to the abandoned mine behind them, Morton being sure to lock it. "Definitely don't want some little kid wandering around in there."

Morton led the way along the edge of the river, ten times the speed of the boats they passed, to an emergency exit. Henry bought a jumbo fluff of Coffin Candy before they parted ways.

"There'll always be an opening at the Uncanny Club for you

two. We'll meet again," Morton said and disappeared back into Botsworth Fun Park.

Henry turned to Lang. "RIP after school tomorrow?"

"Fine," he said and walked away with his hands in his pockets.

"Oh. By the way, Hattie, I told Jacoby Dread you would have a tea party with him."

"You what?"

The Grimworld was colder than it had been in months. Henry and Lang sat huddled in a rigatoni booth over two large steaming fettuccine alfredo plates, avoiding eye contact.

"So. What's next on the list?" Henry said.

Lang focused on cutting his pasta thoroughly. "There's worms and Red Beryl."

"What exactly is Red Beryl?"

"I think it's like a rock."

"Okay, where would we find it?" Lang shrugged and Henry twirled his fork around and around, thinking. "There's not any gem or rock stores around here. Maybe in the Antumbra Region?"

Lang looked up from his pasta. "Remember Madam Desmona? She had all kinds of stones and things on her table."

"Oh right, there were tons of them."

"Maybe she has Red Beryl."

They ate for a few minutes in silence. "So..." Henry began. "Why don't you care about dying?"

Lang continued to focus on his pasta. "It's not that I don't care, I'm just accepting it as a possibility. We're all going to anyway, I just might die sooner."

"But why did you stop looking for a way to reverse it?"

"I don't know."

"You said you liked science, right?"

"I don't know, Henry."

"What about your dad?"

Lang thudded his fork on the table. "It's kind of hard to get your motivation back when your brother dies, alright?"

Henry stared across the table at Lang for a few seconds and looked down at his plate. "Oh."

"I could have saved him but I didn't."

"It wasn't your fault Harlan died."

Lang stared at his plate.

"I'm sorry about your brother, Lang. But don't you understand how terrible it would be for your dad to lose you too? And if we don't figure out how to get these watches off and you die because of it, I'll feel the same way you do right now about Harlan. That I could have done more or tried harder."

Lang was quiet for a long minute, then met Henry's eyes. "Okay, I get it."

"We don't have much time left. Let's go."

They hurried through the cold, still air to Madam Desmona's. From the waiting area, they could hear Madam Desmona's gravelly murmurs punctuated by the high pitched wailing of a woman. A few minutes later a lady ran by them with a look of terror on her face. The boys looked at each other, shuffling their feet uneasily. Desmona's voice reached out from the reading room, beckoning them in. They entered and the orbs hanging on the ceiling greeted them with a twinkle. The crow fluffed its wings. They took a seat around the table and Henry looked at the many stones and gems that decorated the room, some red.

"Boys, so glad to be seeing you again. Did you find Rodney?" Madam Desmona wore a dress of billowy yellow fabric that seemed to float away from her body, making her appear twice her normal size. The spider web tattoo on her face was decorated with tiny purple jewels.

"We did. He helped us a lot," Henry said. "By the way, when was the last time you saw him?"

"Oh, it's been decades."

"Just wondering. Anyway, we came here because we need something."

"What would that be? Do you need your fortune told again?"

"No, we're looking for something called Red Beryl. I think it's a kind of rock."

"You are correct. In fact, I have a piece right on this table." She picked up a small, red cylinder, its translucent sheen glinting in the candlelight. "It was found in the Umbra Region. I've had it for years, but I could let you borrow it."

"That's the thing, it wouldn't be just to borrow."

"Whatever would you do with it?"

"We would need to use it for getting the watches off. Permanently."

Desmona smiled to herself. "I see. I'll tell you what, I could use two boys like yourselves to help me with something. You give me a hand, and I'll give you the Beryl."

"Sure, anything. What do you want?"

"My feet have been very sore lately. Every time I stand up, they ache. My masseuse cancelled today, but since you're here..." The orbs above her trembled in warning.

"You want a foot massage?" Henry said.

"That would be so lovely." She scooted her chair back and peeled off her purple socks to reveal cracked, yellow feet covered in splotchy fungus. She plopped her heels on a small stool.

Their eyes grew wide.

"Seriously?" Henry said under his breath.

"What's the hold-up, boys?" Madam Desmona wiggled her callused toes in anticipation.

"Just do it," Lang muttered. "I'll take the left, you take the right."

"That's not fair, the right has more fungus."

Madam Desmona sighed heavily. "Do you want the Beryl or not?"

They begrudgingly dropped to their knees and reached out for her feet, a vinegary aroma hitting their noses. Henry held his breath, closed his eyes, and rubbed her right foot.

"The pressure is too light, really dig in, boys."

Henry grimaced and looked over at Lang's scrunched up face. After minutes of pretending they were rubbing something, *anything* else, they looked up to find Madam Desmona with her eyes shut and shoulders slouched.

"She fell asleep," Henry whispered.

"I think we've done enough. Let's take the Beryl and get out."

"Won't disagree."

Madam Desmona let out a deep, gurgling snore, and they quietly left the room with the stone in Lang's pocket. The orbs flashed in goodbye.

"We need disinfectant, stat," Henry said once they were back out in the cold.

Lang wiped his hands on his pants in a desperate attempt for cleanliness. "No time for that. Earlier you said you had a way to get worms?"

"Yeah," he said solemnly.

They soon found themselves standing motionless, staring straight ahead.

"This is possibly the worst thing we've had to do yet," Henry said in front of the worm lady's house.

"Why's that?"

"Because I hate worms. They're all slimy and wriggly."

"And yet you love spaghetti."

"Completely different."

They stood immobile.

"You go first." Henry finally said, giving Lang a nudge.

"She sounds creepy. What if the door opens and she's just sitting there with her box, waiting for us?"

They stood some more.

"What if she has worms in her teeth?"

"Lang!" Henry shouted.

"Alright, alright, fine, I'll go," Lang said and went up the steps onto the porch. He knocked once on the door and it opened to reveal the wrinkled, puffed face of the worm lady. A large nightcrawler poked out from her hair.

"What do you want?" She barked and spied Henry behind him. "I told you, boy, I'm not giving my babies to that mongrel."

Henry stepped next to Lang and squared his shoulders. "We're not here on Frank's behalf."

"What, then?"

"Well, my friend Lang here actually has a huge interest in worms."

She eyed him suspiciously.

"We were wondering if you wouldn't mind possibly giving him one, maybe two?"

"So you can dissect them like they do in that school of yours? I think not."

"No, no," Henry said. "To keep as a pet. Because Lang loves worms, don't you Lang?" He elbowed him in the side.

"Yeah, they're the best."

She glared. "What do you like about them?"

"Well, they're really slimy. And wriggly. And if you cut them in half they keep living. Not that I would do that, of course. They're just... really... cute."

The worm lady's eyes lit up. "Aren't they, though?" She opened her door all the way. "All those little segments, the way they move, it's so adorable."

"Yeah, definitely. And they're so... brownish red."

"Just like Muck Cream! Won't you come in?"

They both stepped forward, but she put her hand up in front of Henry. "Not Frank's messenger boy. You wait out here."

"My name is Henry."

She slammed the door in his face, but not before Lang looked back, alarmed. Henry sat on the porch steps and tried to keep warm by the heat given off from the ectolantern. Henry paced back and forth on the porch, worried. Lang hadn't emerged yet. He took a few deep breaths and went to open the door. Before his hand reached the handle, the door burst open to Lang holding a small brown box similar to that the worm lady.

"Now remember they love banana skins. No acidic fruit, though," the worm lady said.

"Yes, ma'am."

"Have a good day now, Langley, and keep me updated on their wellbeing."

She went back inside and Henry backed away down the sidewalk. "Keep that box away from me."

"What, you don't want to hold one?"

"Not in a million years. What was it like in there?"

Lang's eyes widened. "Worms. Lots and lots of worms."

Henry shuddered. "Now we're just waiting on Persi for Zap Sap. And we need hair from Jacoby and Greta, wherever she is. We have to find her."

"I'll try asking around. Let's plan on paying a visit to Jacoby soon."

Later that night, Henry was pulled out of a deep sleep by a noise in his room. He glanced at the alarm clock. Midnight. A pang of fear twisted his stomach and he sat upright, expecting to see a shadowy figure before him, or even worse, the cold, dead eyes of Ferdinand.

"Good, you're up."

Hattie, dressed in black and white checkered pajamas was there instead.

He exhaled. "Thanks to you. It's almost midnight, what are you doing?"

"Did you forget? It's the Smokebrights."

"Can we skip this year?" he said, falling back onto his pillow.

She ripped off his blanket. "Absolutely not."

"Fine. But just for a little while."

She dragged him by the arm to the front door. They opened it and were met with wet streets and misty air. Henry stepped outside barefoot, the bottom of his pajamas instantly wet from the rain puddles.

"My feet are freezing."

She ignored him and skipped through the alley to the main street. Henry followed with grudging footsteps.

The damp air absorbed the buzz of the street lamps and all was quiet. There were no cars, as everyone knew what night it was. They stepped into the middle of the road.

"Look, there are the Dhoul twins. And the Snibbles." Hattie pointed to the children who had come out for the same reason they had.

Henry was about to go back inside but saw the mist in the air flurry and puff.

"Here they come," Hattie said, looking up.

Dozens of purple lights from the Smokebrights appeared against the black sky through the crowded Grimworld buildings. They looped and bobbed and shook, making their way towards the children. Henry could now see the gray smoke-like plumes the lights emitted that slowly disappeared in the mist.

A horn blasted through the streets, and a Botsworth Tram chugged into view on the railway above their house. A group of Smokebrights zipped to the tram and danced along the compartments, hitching a ride. A tram guard popped his head out the window to watch them float along and wave at the children. A few Smokebrights dipped down to the street and brushed between Hattie and Henry. An electric chill went up his spine.

"Big one," Hattie shouted as a large purple light grazed the top of their heads and made their hair stand with static electricity.

"Hey, weren't they orange last year?" Henry said.

"I think it changes."

A few remaining Smokebrights twirled in the mist and sped off to catch up with the Tram. The Dhoul twins ran to follow them but stopped when the last Smokebright's light disappeared. The streets went back to normal, and Henry noticed his toes were going numb.

"Wasn't that fun?" Hattie said and started for the house.

"I'm freezing," he shouted after her.

Back inside he rubbed his hands together and hopped up and down, his feet stinging from the cold. He dove into bed and wrapped himself in his blanket, still tingling from the effect of the Smokebrights. The baby Spotted Harvestmen were in a container on his bedside table, well fed and growing. He watched them scurry about, and once he was sufficiently warm, he curled up and fell asleep.

Chapter 11

Mothball Grocer's Special Toilet

After a particularly boring day at school the next day, Henry was finishing up his homework when there was a knock on his door. Gobbert stepped in.

"Hey Hen, there's someone outside to see you. Says his name is Jacoby Dread."

Henry shot up from his desk chair. "I've got it, Dad."

"Who is-"

Before Gobbert had the chance to finish, Henry was in the kitchen and out the door. He abruptly came face to face with Jacoby, who was dressed in a heavy trench coat. His face was snug between a red scarf and his bowler hat. Ferdinand stood behind him, tall and stoic.

"Henry, if you would come for a walk we have a matter to discuss," Jacoby said.

"Can we do this later?"

"No. I've waited long enough. Now come along."

Henry quickly closed the door behind him before Gobbert came. They strolled through the crisp, dark gray streets, his sweater not nearly enough in the cold.

Jacoby kept his gaze ahead of him, hands planted in his pockets. "I was promised a tea party," he said.

"I know, Hattie's just been really busy."

He glanced at Henry with weary eyes. "You would think an 11-year-old would be able to make time in her schedule."

"Well, it's just going to have to wait."

"What if I told you I have information you want?"

Henry slowed down. "What information?"

"I do recall you asking if I knew a Miss Greta Flingbossom. I've recently come across the name and I believe I know where you can find her."

"Really? Where?"

"Ah, ah, first the tea party."

"Tomorrow after school. She'll be at your manor. Now tell me."

"I'll send her home with the information."

Henry sighed. "Fine."

"Be gone."

Henry stopped walking and watched Jacoby and Ferdinand continue on their way. Back at home, he found his dad waiting in the kitchen.

"I thought there was a Fiendfire the way you flew out here," Gobbert said.

"Sorry, Dad. That was someone from Frank's to talk to me about Spotted Harvestman."

"I see."

"By the way, could you bring home a couple Botsworth Bars from the candy factory tomorrow? I've been wanting one."

"Sure thing, Hen. I'll bring some of the new Fingernail Gummies, too. They just came out with a new lemon yellow nail polish."

Hattie strolled into the kitchen in search of an after dinner snack.

"Hey, I got a cool comic book I want to show you," Henry said, motioning for her to come to his room.

She looked at him suspiciously but followed. He closed the door behind her. "Guess what you get to do tomorrow?"

"What?"

"Tea party with Jacoby Dread."

Her eyes narrowed. "I was hoping he'd forget."

"Well, now he has information we need and the only way to get it is for you to just drink a little tea with the man."

"You're the worst brother ever."

"I'll take you there after school tomorrow. I'm sure you'll

have a jolly good time." He stuck his pinky out and pretended to drink from a teacup.

She tapped his hand. "This better help you out, *a lot*."

The next day after school Hattie packed her dolls into a suitcase and they headed for Sable Avenue.

"Henry and Hattie Bats," Henry said to the two guards at the gate. They let them through, and Hattie bumped her suitcase behind her along the cobbled pathway. She was immediately in awe of the Manor.

"Look at that fountain. And this house. You didn't tell me Jacoby owned a mansion."

"Yeah, yeah, he's a greedy creep with a lot of money."

"I can't believe this."

They stepped up to the giant doors and Henry paused. "Before we go in, there's something else I need you to do."

"This isn't enough?"

"It's important. I need you to get a strand of his hair."

"I am not touching his hair."

"You will if you want your brother to live past twenty. The only thing is, he's always wearing a hat so just tell him to take it off because, I don't know, that's what people do at tea parties."

"You owe me big time."

"I appreciate your cooperation."

Henry thumped the knocker and the door was opened by Ferdinand. "Mr Henry Bats and Ms Hattie Bats, I presume."

Henry nodded and Ferdinand took the suitcase from Hattie. "Please follow me." They stepped forward, but Ferdinand held his hand. "Only Hattie may proceed."

"Then what am I supposed to do?"

"Whatever you please."

He shrugged and watched Hattie disappear upstairs. He decided he would wander the Manor but quickly found out the halls were teeming with guards who were not keen on him exploring. He did manage to get into the kitchen, which was filled with bustling chefs and waiters going in and out with dessert trays filled to the brim. He snatched a Gloop Scoop, returned to the foyer, and sat on a waiting bench.

Nearly an hour had passed and Henry fell soundly asleep on the uncomfortable bench. Something slapped his cheek and he sat up, startled. Hattie was before him with daggers for eyes.

"We're leaving," she said and rolled her suitcase out the door.

Henry wiped some drool from his chin and caught up. "How'd it go?"

"There were desserts. Hundreds of desserts. And chairs for Every. Single. Doll."

"Did you have fun?"

"My doll collection is important to me, but I don't think they're alive. He gave them voices, Henry. Voices." She shuddered. "He invited me to some kind of ball he's having, too."

"Anything else you have to tell me?"

"I don't know if you deserve it. I had to eat five Cobweb Cakes and I think I'm going to puke."

"It's for a good cause."

"I suppose it is. I made him take off his hat and there was a hair in there. I just picked it off. It's in Mabelle's pocket."

"Nice going. Anything else?"

"He said you might be able to find the person you're looking for at the 'Pampuzzle League.' He's not sure where their current headquarters are since he's been dead for a bit, but word is they've been meeting at the grocery store on Mothball Lane."

"That's exactly the information I needed. Thanks, Hattie." He thumped her on the shoulder.

"I expect at least three new dolls for my birthday."

"I'll find the most demented ones I can."

"I think you owe me that much."

"No come on, I think we've found Greta."

They hurried home and Henry gave Lang a call. "Great news."

"What's that?" Lang said.

"Hattie got Jacoby's hair, and he gave me the location of where we might be able to find Greta Flingbossom. We'll have to go to a grocery store."

"A grocery store?"

"Yeah, I'll explain later. Meet me at the one on Mothball Lane."

Armed with safety scissors in case they had the opportunity to snip some hair, they met up at Mothball Grocers. The fruit section in front contained several bruised and rotten apples and nearly all the peaches had been stuck with someone's thumb. They wandered the store and asked a worker named Alfreda, who was stocking alfredo sauce, about the Pampuzzle League. She furrowed her eyebrows.

"Is that a kind of mustard?" she said in a gravelly voice.

"Uh, no. It's some kind of club that's supposed to be here."

"Never heard of it, kid." She moved down the aisle to stock soup.

"So much for help from Alfreda. Now what?"

"If Jacoby Dread is familiar with this league, it must be pretty exclusive. I'm guessing there's a secret entrance, something like that," Lang said.

They scavenged the grocery's black linoleum floors and red walls in search of a trap door. They found nothing odd, but Henry did spy a squared spaghetti ball, which he mentally noted to ask Mildred to buy.

"Now what?" Lang said.

"Keep looking, we're not leaving until we find something."

Henry was in the middle of inspecting the tuna section when they noticed a man who looked rather out of place. He was wearing an expensive pea soup colored coat and a black top hat, which covered his downcast eyes.

"Lang, look," Henry said and nodded his head towards the man.

"Looks suspicious, definitely doesn't live around here. Let's follow him."

They trailed behind, watching the man do a lap around aisle 11, then 4, and 16, stopping briefly to look at a few clam broth cans before moving on. Finally, when he saw no one else around, he approached cash register two. Henry and Lang crouched down behind a watermelon crate and watched intently. The man made a subtle hand signal to the cashier by crossing his pointer finger and thumb. The cashier, a man with a puff of brown curly hair, calmly handed the man a tiny metal object that reflected the light. The mysterious man then doubled back and headed straight for where Henry and Lang were hiding. They stumbled back and stood upright, pretending to have a sudden fascination with toothpaste. The man passed them, and as soon as he rounded a corner, they followed him towards the bathrooms.

"Why didn't we think of the bathrooms?" Henry said.

"Why would anyone put a secret door in a bathroom?"

"Apparently it was a good decision."

The man disappeared into the bathroom and they slowly opened the door and peeked through. He was nowhere to be seen, but a strange shifting noise came from one of the five stalls.

"Looks like we found the entrance," Lang said.

"I just can't believe it's by a toilet."

"First we have to get whatever that metal thing was."

"I think you should do it. You look more authoritative."

"How does a 14-year-old look authoritative?"

"I don't know, you're tall?"

Lang went back to the cash register and tried to keep his shoulders back and stand as straight as possible. Henry watched from behind the watermelons.

"Are you purchasing anything today, sir?" the cashier said.

Lang cleared his throat and glanced down to his hand, which was in the pointer finger over thumb position. The cashier stared for a moment at his fingers and looked back up. He slowly reached under the conveyer belt and pulled out a key, handing it to Lang, who briefly nodded and walked away.

"Nice," Henry said.

"Thanks."

They went into the men's bathroom and opened the first stall. Nothing out of the ordinary except for a bit of toilet paper on the floor. They went to the second. "Ew, someone forgot to flush."

The third, however, had an out of order sign. They bent down and looked beneath the gap. Empty. Henry pushed the door open and on the other side, they found a tiny nick in the tiled wall, just big enough for a key to fit. Lang stuck the key in and a short, silent rumble followed. The back stall tiles, along with the toilet, pushed back to reveal a passage.

"Daddy, did you hear that?" came the voice of a boy two stalls down.

"Someone had too many raspberries, son."

Henry and Lang stepped through and the stall wall moved back into place with a click. Before them was a concrete staircase that ended at a large steel door. They approached, and a metal slider opened to reveal two dark eyes peering through. "Password?" spoke a low growl.

"We didn't figure out the password," Henry whispered.

"I know, I know."

"I ain't got all day, especially for a couple of kids."

Henry stepped forward. "Uh, Pampuzzle?"

"Get lost, kids."

The slider slammed shut.

"Pampuzzle? Really?" Lang said.

Henry shrugged. "Guess we're stuck until we figure a way in."

They sat next to the door for what seemed like ages until the toilet swung back around and a man dressed in a shiny red suit walked down the stairs. He did a double take at the boys and knocked on the door.

The slider opened and the voice asked for the password. The

man leaned in and whispered, Henry straining to hear what he said. All he made out was, "A toilet stall, unbelievable," as the door opened and the man passed through.

"Aw, come on," Henry said.

"We'll get in eventually."

The next person that arrived was an elderly fellow dressed in a trench coat and sporting a long gray beard. He looked down at them with a twinkle in his eyes, one was green, the other completely white.

"Who do we have here, a couple of whippersnappers looking to get into the Pampuzzle League?" he smiled widely.

"Well, we're trying," Henry said. "We don't know the password."

The man nodded. "That darn thing changes so much I can hardly keep track. But I'll help you out this time, eh? 'Spoiled Pudding' is this week's moniker. Enjoy, boys."

After he went through, they stood up and knocked on the door.

"Not you two again. I thought I told you to scram," the voice said.

"Spoiled Pudding," Henry stated.

The man rolled his eyes. "Did that coot give out the password again? Fine, come in. But behave yourselves, or I'll personally kick you out."

He opened the door and they entered another world.

The Pampuzzle League was a large room filled with dining tables and people dressed in lavish clothing. They were a cheery group, chatting loudly and laughing with one another. Henry stepped onto red, plush carpet and looked up, dazzled by an enormous, sparkling chandelier. A woman dressed in a black jeweled dress, her hair pinned with crystal clips, played a lolling tune on a grand piano. Waiters carrying silver trays piled with finger foods made their rounds.

"What is this place?" Lang said.

Henry looked around, wide-eyed. "Somewhere Jacoby would definitely hang out."

They backed away to the edge of the room and scanned the crowd, but saw no one who looked like the picture of Greta Flingbossom from the death record.

"She might not be here, you know," Lang said.

"Come on, let's keep looking."

They made their way to the center of the room, receiving several glances and glares.

"I saw Jacoby out and about the other day," Henry heard a woman draped in furs say.

"Back from the dead again?" a man in a pinstripe suit responded. "How does he do it?"

"I heard he's hosting a Return Ball."

They spotted the old man who had helped them with the password. He was standing with a group of people, laughing heartily.

"Maybe we should ask him," Henry said.

"Worth a try."

They sidled up to the old man and politely waited for him to notice them. Eventually, his green eye wandered over to the misplaced guests and he grinned widely.

"Ah, the door boys," he exclaimed. "Brutus didn't give you any trouble, did he?"

"No, he let us in," Henry said.

"Grand. Is there something else you need from me?"

"Yeah, actually we're looking for someone named Greta Flingbossom."

"Greta, eh? You'll find the lady over there, drinking her usual Bloody Carrie."

He pointed to the bar, where a woman wearing a long red dress and white gloves with her hair in a bun sat facing away from them.

"Thank you."

"Anytime, anytime."

They made their way over to the bar. "Ready, Lang?"

"Ready."

Chapter 12

House of Squishy Seats

Henry and Lang sat on the stools on each side of the woman in red, and they could see why they weren't able to recognize Greta from the death record. She looked about fifty years older. Her skin was a papery white with sharp, sunken features and her scalp was barely covered by thin, light gray hair. Her figure looked skeletal and weak, but she maintained an upright posture. She looked to her right with cutting eyes and saw Henry, and then to her left and saw Lang. She jumped and put her hand to her heart.

"Is that you, Langley?"

He nodded. "Hello, Mrs Flingbossom."

"What are you doing here? How did you find me?"

"My friend Henry and I were able to track you down."

She began to stand up, but Lang did as well. "Wherever you go, I go."

She huffed and sat back down. "I can have you kicked out, you know." She jutted her chin up and stared ahead at a painting of dogs playing darts behind the bar. "Whatever you came here for, I'm not giving you a single thing. So you may as well leave."

"I'm not here to ask you for anything."

"Then what do you want?"

"I just want to know why you did it."

She looked at him with a sharp turn of her neck. "See, there's something you want, right there. You want answers." Lang glanced at Henry, who nodded and pulled out the safety scissors. "And it's none of your business."

She turned her head forward and Henry recoiled before she saw him.

"Don't you think I have a right to know? You stole part of my lifespan," Lang said, keeping his tone even.

She looked at him again. "It used to be your lifespan, it's mine now."

Henry made his move and snipped off a stray hair from her bun. He plucked it off her dress and gave Lang the thumbs up.

"My brother is already gone, you know," Lang said. "And as I'm sure you're aware, I don't have much time left either."

Greta cleared her throat and stared at the painting. "My husband and I wished to become immortal. That is all."

"So your husband was the one who used my brother?"

"Yes. He's currently in Vytiper form, searching for another."

Lang looked down and nodded. "Another, huh? Well, that was all that I came for."

She pursed her lips and Lang stood up. They went to leave the Pampuzzle League.

"That's all you're going to say to her?" Henry said.

"There's nothing I could have said that would change anything." Lang's eyes darkened. "So let's just make sure she doesn't do it again."

He sped toward a side exit, with Henry close behind, and as they passed yet another bodyguard, the man gave them a strange look. They went up a flight of concrete stairs to a button at the top that pushed out the toilet and they quickly found out why the guard had given them the odd look. Back under the stall, they were met with a mother and daughter standing at the sink, washing their hands. They were in the girl's bathroom. The mother spotted the boys in the mirror and spun around. "Scoundrels, unruly children!" she yelled, swinging her purse at them. They hurried out to the safety of the produce section.

"Glad we got out of there," Henry said.

"The League or the bathroom?"

"Both. But we got Greta's hair at least."

Henry was at the table doing homework when Mildred

flitted by.

"Your friend Persi called, Hen. She wants you to call her back as soon as possible. We should really invite her over."

"Thanks, Mom."

When all was clear, he dialed Persi's number. "Hey it's Henry, you called?"

"I got the Zap Sap, but you'll have to come to my house to pick it up. I'm grounded."

"What did you do?"

"I snuck out to the Shady Phantom last night and got caught. My parents are so controlling, they never let me have any fun."

"Okay, I'll be over in a few."

"When you get there just tell my mom you go to Leechy High."

She gave Henry her address and he told Mildred he was going over to Persi's house to pick something up for school.

Persi's home was a peach colored, two-story row house smooshed between a series of other pastel houses that stood out against the gray backdrop. Henry rang the doorbell, and it was answered by a woman who looked similar to Persi, only less colorful, and much, much rounder. She wore a long-sleeved pale orange dress. Persi's mother.

"Persimmon told me she was expecting company," she said, her face puckered and devoid of a smile. "She's finishing up her homework, so you'll have to come inside and wait."

She walked Henry to the parlor and he sat on the couch. The cushions were large and squishy, and he found himself sinking into them. A case nearby was filled with glass oranges, and the room was orderly and pristine.

He could feel the woman's penetrating gaze and found himself struggling for something to say. Finally, she spoke.

"Henry, what school do you go to?"

"Leechy High," he said.

"But you're clearly not in the same grade, how did you meet

Persimmon?"

He paused for a moment and pulled out the pocket watch. "We just walked past each other and she stopped to ask where I got this."

"So you're the one that started that," she said, her face squeezed together like she had bit into a lemon.

"They're really popular in school. I'm sure she would have gotten one anyway," he said, wishing to disappear into the couch.

He heard thumping on the staircase and Persi burst into the parlor, a vibrant streak of color. Her hair was red and yellow this time and she wore patched rainbow overalls over a lime green shirt.

"I'm done with my homework, Mother. Henry will just be here for a minute to discuss tutoring. Come on up, Henry."

He nodded in respect to her mom, and she stared back with suspicious eyes. Upstairs Persi opened the door to her room, which was the complete opposite of the rest of the house. Clothes and empty pizza boxes covered every surface, and CDs and makeup lined every shelf. The walls were covered with band posters illuminated by a purple lava lamp, and everything was splattered with an array of every imaginable color of hair dye.

"You like?" she asked and kicked the clothes pile out of the way to make a path. "You can sit in the beanbag over there."

Henry sat in the giant beanbag chair, enveloped much as he had been on the couch. Persi put on some music and shuffled through the contents of a dresser. Eventually, she pulled out a little plastic bag with a small yellow substance inside.

"Here's the Zap Sap. Sorry, there's still a little blood on it."

"That's okay."

"So what have you and Lang been up to?"

"Well, we've got everything now. My dad gave me the Botsworth Bars this morning." He heard a shuffle from underneath the clothes pile. "What's that?"

"Oh, that's just my hamster, Thrasher. He runs wild around here. I like to give him that freedom." Persi flopped onto her bed and started chipping absently at her purple fingernails. "So I found my Vytiper."

"Really?"

"Yeah, I did some digging around. Her name is Vilma Spreebust. She's super cool, rides a motorbike. Awesome chick."

Henry stared at her. "You think she's awesome? You're not mad at her?"

"Nah, she did what she had to do."

"No good person would consider taking someone else's life for their own."

"Well, she had a lot of life yet to live. Died real young in a bike accident. The Vytiper thing was her back up. Said she found out how to do it from her sister, Greta."

"Greta?" He shook his head. "Doesn't matter. Anyway, that's no excuse."

"I guess you're right. But that doesn't stop me from liking her."

Henry rolled his eyes. "Whatever you believe. You just need to get a strand of her hair."

"Pink," Persi said.

"What?"

"Her hair is pink. Maybe I should dye my hair pink." She examined her fingernails thoughtfully.

"I'm going to go now. Thanks for the Sap, and good luck with your hair."

"You don't want to stay? I got a new Vile Croquettes CD."

"Nah, I should get going, I've got a lot of homework."

"Alright, later Henry."

"Later, Persi."

He went back downstairs where Persi's mother was waiting at the bottom, arms crossed. She opened the door and Henry hurried out. He heard the door slam loudly behind him.

"I've got all the ingredients, I just got back from Persi's," Henry told Lang on the telephone as soon as he got back home.

"Really? So we're all set?"

"Yeah. Is your dad around tomorrow after school?"

"No, he's working late."

"Perfect. Hang tight." Henry grasped his watch hard in his fist. "We're getting these things off."

Chapter 13

Ferdinand Purchases Floss

Howlers' Tunnel stretched out before Henry and Lang.

"Want to race?" Henry grinned.

"You're on."

"On three. One... two... hey, no fair!" Henry called as Lang sprinted forward before he had a chance to count to three.

He raced through the tunnel, barely hearing the voices that tried to echo in his mind. Their footsteps rang through the concrete, Henry's legs pumping beneath him. He reached the end to see Lang, who was waiting, arms crossed, foot tapping.

"Too slow."

"You cheated."

"Just a little."

They ran the rest of the way to Lang's house. Inside, they lined up the odd assortment of things they had collected and reviewed the rhyme the GrimMan had given them. Lang found two large pots and set them on a burner. "One for you, one for me. Alright, first let's steep the Botsworth Bars."

"What's steep?" Henry said.

"It means we need to soak them in boiling water."

They filled the pots and turned the heat up until steam moistened their faces and the water bubbled and popped. Henry unwrapped the Botsworth bars to reveal the brown bars studded with green globs. He carefully dropped them in the boiling water.

"We'll need to wait a bit," Lang said.

They stood over the pots and watched the chocolate bars turn the water brown.

"So this is it," Henry said. "We'll get our life back in just a few minutes."

"What do you think will happen to Jacoby and Greta?"

"The rhyme says they'll meet their maker. But they've already died before, so I don't feel too bad."

Lang turned to look at Henry. "So, hey…"

"Hm?"

"I've decided in the future I want to research entities. You know, to help kids like us."

Henry smiled. "Lang, that's great. Maybe I'll even help you."

"Yeah." He smiled too and looked at the pots. "Alright, now all we have to do is add the rest of the ingredients."

"*A piece of Red Beryl and a sprig of Boosprit,*" Henry read.

Lang smashed the Red Beryl into two pieces with a hammer and they sunk to the bottom of the pots. "Boosprit," he said.

Henry handed him the sprigs and they sizzled and shrunk as they hit the boiling water.

"*A Spotted Harvestman and Zap Sap, just a bit.*"

Lang opened the bag for the yellow Zap Sap and let it ooze into the pots, each drop producing an electric spark.

"Now the Harvestmen, sorry little guys." Henry opened the container and dropped one in each pot. "Now, *Hair from the Vytiper, blood of the reaped, one part worm.* Lang, the worms."

Lang looked inside the box the worm lady had given him. "Goodbye Squish. Goodbye Squirm."

"You named them?"

"I don't know, they kind of grew on me."

"Maybe your future is as the Worm Man."

"Can you put them in? I don't know if I can do it."

Henry nodded and reluctantly took the box. He held it as far away from him as possible and used a set of tongs to dump them into each pot. "It's over, you can look now."

They let Jacoby and Greta's hair float down into each of their pots and curl with the heat. Lang took out a kitchen knife from a drawer. "Now we just need our blood."

After a minute of hesitation, Henry twisted the knife into his finger and the red liquid fell into his pot. The brew turned bright red and faded to a black darker than the Grimworld sky. It bubbled and steamed furiously until the concoction coagulated into a thick goo the size of a skipping stone. Lang did the same.

"The Dirt Adalis that almost ate us, the worm lady, rubbing Madam Desmona's feet. All that work for just a little bit of goo," Henry said, poking it with a spoon. "But we definitely did it right."

"Yeah, there's no way all of that would have turned into a putty ball." Lang unscrewed the crown of his watch. "Just one more step."

Henry felt his heart race as he unscrewed his. "This is it." He picked up the tiny black blob and rolled it around in his fingers. "In it goes in three...two...one."

The blob fit perfectly in the watch chamber and they twisted the cap back on.

"Last part," Lang said. *"Set back time to 12 o'clock, and only then shall the watches fall off."*

They set their fingers on the minute hand and pushed clockwise. Only, the minute hand wouldn't budge.

"Lang, is yours still stuck?"

"Yeah."

"That's weird." Henry reviewed the rhyme. "We did everything according to what the GrimMan said. All the ingredients are there, we steeped the Botsworth Bar, and it all turned into that gel." He smacked the rhyme paper onto the counter. "This is ridiculous."

"Why does it smell like burning worms in here?" came a voice from the living room. Barnaby Skullfield walked into the kitchen with a bundle of grocery bags loaded in his arms. He stopped when he found the two hovered over their pots, examining their watches.

"Dad, you're home early," Lang said, dropping the watch on his chest with a plunk.

"Are you guys," he sniffed the air, "trying to cook?"

"Science experiment," Lang said.

"Just don't burn the apartment down. Good to see you again, Henry." Barnaby set the groceries on the counter. "I got off work early, thought we could have dinner together. Henry, would you like to join us?"

"Sure, I just need to call my mom."

"I'll clean this up," Lang said.

Henry called Mildred.

"Oh, you're having dinner with Lang? That's wonderful," her voice pierced through the phone.

"I'll be back after."

He hung up and helped Lang wash out the pots "Now what?" he whispered, Barnaby sat in the living room reading a book.

"I don't know." Lang glanced back through the kitchen to his dad with a somber expression. "But we have to get these off no matter what."

"Right. We'll think of something."

They finished tidying up the kitchen and Barnaby took over. "I got some frozen dinners, and for dessert, blood pudding." He popped the dinners in the oven and set the table. When everything was ready they all sat down. The room now smelled like burnt worms and mini cornslogs.

"This looks great, Mr Skullfield," Henry said.

"Thank you, Henry. And you can call me Barnaby. Go ahead, dig in."

The contents of the unfrozen dinner were squishy and slightly melted, but good.

"I have to tell you, I'm so glad Lang became friends with a nice boy like yourself."

Henry and Lang looked at each other. "Well, I'm glad to be friends with Lang."

"My boy's a good one. So tell me, what do your parents do for a living?"

"My dad works at Gelatin Skeleton and my mom is at Coffin Werks Funeral Home. What do you do?"

"This and that, whatever work I can get. Sometimes a gas station attendant, most of the time a bus driver. Once I worked in the cafeteria at your school."

"Oh, I think I remember you. You served the mashed peas?"

"That's right. I tried to add some spices but they wouldn't let me."

"It must be cool having so many jobs."

"It is. Just today I was driving my bus route and out of nowhere, this giant truck tire came rolling down the road. Nearly hit the thing, but I was able to swerve onto the sidewalk without running into anyone. Oh and yesterday at the gas station there was a customer with a Twiddlefit attached to her shoulder."

"A Twiddlefit?"

"Yep, it was latched right on. You could only see it when she talked. Nice lady, though."

"I wonder if it feels like a Twiddleknit attachment."

"Exactly what I thought."

When it came time to say goodbye, Henry thanked them both.

"You be sure to come over another time. It was great fun."

"I will."

Lang walked him outside the apartment building.

"I'll visit Jacoby soon, see if anything's changed," Henry said. "Although I don't think it has."

They both stared at the ground.

"The minute hand is getting really close to the one."

Henry looked up. "I won't let you die. I'll let you know as soon as I've thought of something."

Henry sat at his desk and read the rhyme over and over.

"We did everything," he mumbled to himself. "*With a hand from the Vytiper.* That's got to be the hair we got from them. But we still can't turn back time. What do we need to turn back time?

Do we need the Vytiper's actual hand?" He shoved the paper off his desk and put his head in his hands. "What do I do? Come on, Henry, Lang's counting on me. I can't give up now."

He stood up and left his room.

"Hen, where are you off to?" Mildred said from the living room couch.

He was heading to Jacoby Dread's.

"Just Frank's."

"Could you stop at the grocery and pick up eggs for dinner?"

"What are we having?"

"Blackened Quiche."

"Sure, Mom."

He decided to stop at Mothball Grocers, as it was only a few blocks from Sable Avenue. He asked Alfeda where the eggs were and walked to aisle 16. A woman dressed in a silk coat and fruit bat hat passed him by, surely a member of the Pampuzzle League. Eggs in hand, he made his way to the cash register but stopped in his tracks when he glanced down aisle 8.

"Toothpaste," Jacoby Dread said.

Ferdinand studied a row of tubes and dropped one in the basket he held. "They don't have your usual brand, sir, but this is the most expensive."

"So, Jacoby's still around," Henry said to himself.

"Floss."

"Sir, if you would look down the aisle." Ferdinand pointed.

"Is that the Bats boy?" Jacoby said, spying Henry.

"I believe it is."

Henry walked down the aisle. "Shopping in a commoners market today?"

Jacoby briefly looked Henry up and down, and then continued to peruse the dental hygiene section. "You know, just as well as I, that the Pampuzzle League is located here. Tell me, did Hattie enjoy the tea party?"

"Oh, she had a swell time."

"I thought so. I did invite her to my Return Ball, I hope she'll choose to come. You'll be interested to know that Greta Flingbossom will be in attendance, I made her acquaintance just the other day. I'm still not sure how she got her hands on the Vytiper instructions. Ah, they have my floss." He reached up with his one gloved hand and grabbed a container.

"Perhaps you could help me with something, Henry. I've received this edition of the Pampuzzle key, but it appears the secret door location has changed."

"Where did you look?"

"The maintenance closet. Was it not there when you visited?"

"No, it's in the bathroom."

Jacoby's eye twitched. "The bathroom?"

"Yeah, but it has to be the girl's bathroom. Third stall from the left, there's a keyhole."

"Ferdinand, they've resorted to a toilet. Unbelievable. Pay for the groceries and drop them off at the Manor." He waved his hand at Henry. "Continue your shopping, I have business to attend to."

Henry followed Ferdinand to the cash register, keeping a few steps behind the butler. He remembered something from the Vytiper book and his brain was working overtime.

"Hands, watches," Henry murmured. "With a hand from the Vytiper."

They got in line and Henry tapped the butler's cold shoulder. "Ferdinand, did Jacoby lose a glove?"

He turned his neck with a creak to look at the boy. "No, that is the master's style."

"Oh, just curious."

Once Henry paid for the eggs, he hurried home past Frank's, past the worm lady, to his kitchen where the telephone was waiting. He dialed Lang's number.

"Hello?"

"Lang, Jacoby is still alive, er, living, uh, you know what I mean. I don't think the reversal worked all the way, but I think I know what we have to do now."

"Let's hear it."

Chapter 14

Grandpa Flemm's Stuffed Bear

Henry stood in the doorway of his sister's room with his arms crossed. She was rearranging her dolls.

"Hattie, I need you to go to Jacoby's Return Ball."

She whipped around. "You want me to do what?"

"Lang and I got all the ingredients and put them in the watch, but it wasn't enough. We were missing something. The reversal rhyme says *With a hand from the Vytiper*. Have you noticed that Jacoby only wears one glove?"

"Yeah."

"And when we met Greta she was wearing gloves. In the translated book it mentions that the Vytiper has to keep something hidden. I think underneath his glove is the missing hour hand from the pocket watch. I'm guessing I need to get that and reset the time to 12 o'clock."

"Well that's great, but why do I need to go to the ball?"

"Because Greta Flingbossom, Lang's Vytiper, will be there too. This is a perfect opportunity and we need your help."

She perfected her doll alignment and crossed her arms. "I'll do it. I want to keep you around for a little longer. Lang too."

"Thank you, Hattie. You're really saving my life here, literally."

"That's what sisters are for. What do you need me to do?"

"Get us through the gate, since you're the only one invited. Otherwise, I'm not sure yet. Jacoby's got a lot of guards around now, plus Ferdinand. He'll figure out what we're trying to do. Do you think Morton could help?"

"I'll ask. When's the Ball?"

"This weekend. I'm counting on you."

He left her room and snuck past his parents, who were

watching TV, and into the kitchen to make a call.

"Persi, this is Henry," he whispered when she answered.

"What's up? I was just in the middle of dying my hair."

"Pink?"

"You guessed it."

"Are you free this weekend?"

"My mom has a violin lesson set up, why?"

"Lang and I know how to get the watches off, but we need your help."

"What'd you need me to do?"

"We have to get into this Ball and take out our Vytipers."

"A ball? Like one of those stuffy dance parties with fancy clothes?"

"Yeah."

"Ick. You can't just do it yourselves?"

"Maybe, but the more people the better. This'll make us 100% sure how to get the watches off so we can help you, too."

Persi paused for a minute. "Alright, I guess I can get out of my lessons."

"Thanks, Persi, you're the best."

The day before the Return Ball Henry found himself sitting across from Lang at RIP. They dug into a plate of macaroni and examined a diagram they had laid out on the table.

"Okay, here's the plan so far. We're guessing we'll all be able to get past the guards at the gate because they'll know Hattie. Then, Hattie will arrive at the door with her guest, Morton. Even though he's not on the list, I think they'll let him in," Henry said.

"Then they sneak into the dining hall and let me, you, and Persi in through the window. That's all we've got."

"We should get Jacoby and Greta alone, where there aren't any guards. We may have to split up at this point."

"You take Hattie since Jacoby knows her. And she's your sister."

"Alright. Greta may be more trouble so you should take Persi and Morton."

"There are a lot of variables. We'll have to assess the situation to know how we should proceed."

"We should hope for the best, and prepare for the worst. And I hate to say it, but maybe we should wear suits or something so we look like we belong."

"I think you're right."

Henry slurped the last macaroni from his fork. "We all meet at 5 p.m at Frank's, I'll call and let everyone know of the plan."

Lang nodded, and his face looked as serious as Henry had ever seen it. "This is it."

Henry knocked on his grandpa's attic door.

"Who is it?"

"It's Henry."

"Henry?"

"Your grandson."

"Did you bring lettuce?"

"No, Grandpa." He opened the door and his ears filled with the jazzy tune that played on the phonograph. Grandpa Flemm sat in his chair, reading a book on taxidermy.

"What do you want, boy?" He asked, peering over the book and puffing his pipe.

"Do you have an old suit I could borrow?"

"A suit? For what?"

"School dance."

Flemm stared at Henry for a moment with papery eyes and pushed himself up with creaky bones. The man had shrunk with age and was barely taller than Henry. He waddled to a closet behind a bookshelf and shuffled around.

"Take a look at this fellow." He hauled out a stout taxidermy bear in his short arms. The bear was dressed in a tweed suit and hat, its marble eyes flashing in the dim light. "Stuffed this right before the war."

"That's perfect."

Flemm undressed the bear and gave the suit to Henry. "I want this back. And bring lettuce next time, Millie hasn't made a salad in years."

"Will do, Grandpa."

Henry stashed the suit in his room and made the announcement to his parents. "I'll be sleeping over at Lang's tomorrow."

They glanced up at him from the TV. "We had plans to take you and Hattie to the movies," Mildred said.

"Attack of the Giant Thread Spinners 2, you guys really liked the first one," said Gobbert.

Hattie stepped in. "Actually, I have a sleepover tomorrow too."

"Really, with who?"

"Tabitha."

"This Tabitha should really come over to our house for a change," Gobbert said. "Mildred, what do you think?"

"I supposed we can just go to the movies ourselves."

"We'll all go to the movies next week, right, Henry?"

"Right."

"Well, alright. You kids can go to your sleepovers."

Henry went to bed that night knowing everything was in place for the Ball. He patted the pocket watch around his neck. He hardly noticed the weight anymore but tomorrow, if all went well, it would be gone.

In the morning he ate his usual bowl of Sugar Slugs next to Hattie, and they gave each other knowing looks. They watched their regular cartoons so as to not alert their parents of anything suspicious. The day ticked by and Henry paced his room as it became closer to leave, running different scenarios through his head. It was around 4 p.m when his parents left for the movies.

"Bye, love you," they said.

"Bye Mom, bye Dad, love you."

The door closed and he and Hattie bolted for their rooms to get ready. The tweed suit was itchy and uncomfortable, and just a bit too big. He decided to leave the hat behind. Hattie emerged from her room in a long-sleeved black dress, her hair twisted into a bun. "Nice suit," she said. "Where'd you get it, Grandpa Flemm?"

"Yes, actually."

She shrugged. "Figures."

They left the house and entered the dusky streets of Grimworld. The sky was as dark as it had been the night Jacoby had tricked him, and a layer of fog sat on the ground so thick that the headlights of passing cars could barely pierce through. The air was moist and cold, and Henry's skin was instantly covered with goosebumps. They reached Frank's and outside found Lang shifting on his feet, dressed in a dark green suit much too big for him. He apparently had the same idea as Henry. Morton was next to him in a gray pinstripe suit that was much too small.

"Wore this to a funeral when I was nine," he said.

"Alright, everyone's here except Persi." Henry looked up and down the streets until a pink swatch emerged from the fog. Persi's hair glowed like neon. She was dressed in purple from head to toe, her shirt covered with laughing skulls.

"Guess I never gave her the dress code," Henry said.

Persi walked up to them and put her hands on her hips. "You guys look... interesting."

"So do you. This is my sister, Hattie, and her friend, Morton. Are we ready to head out?"

"Ready," everyone agreed.

The group marched through the fog to Sable Avenue. Multiple limousines and even a few horse carriages passed by on their way to Jacoby Dread's. They walked by the cemetery where Jacoby had first led Henry posing as a Nightspook and soon arrived at the end of the street. Two security guards loomed from the mist, waving limousines in. Hattie led the group with her head held high. One guard put his hand up to them.

"I don't think anybody invited a bunch of kids," he said in a gruff voice.

"My name is Hattie Bats, these are my guests."

He dropped his hand. "Oh, Ms Bats. I was told you're a VIP guest. Please come in, my apologies."

"Yes, of course."

They stepped through the gate to Dread Manor. The building glowed with dim gray lights, Ferdinand was checking in a flurry of people at the front door.

Henry pulled his friends aside. "Alright, the mission is to separate Jacoby and Greta and get their gloves off. If my theory is correct, they'll have an hour hand on them somewhere. Get those, and Lang and I will do the rest. The three of us will lay low as long as possible. Hattie and Morton, we'll meet you by the window." Henry, Lang, and Persi scurried out of sight to the side of the manor and hunkered down beneath the dining hall window. After what seemed like ages, the window clicked and lifted up. Hattie stuck her head out. "Sorry, Jacoby was showing me to my private table filled with dolls."

"You serious?" Henry said.

"Deadly."

They hoisted themselves up the window and dropped into the room. "Persi, you should stay back while we lure Greta and Jacoby away," Lang said.

"Why?"

"You just stand out a bit too much. Keep an eye out, we'll try to bring them towards you."

"Operation Takedown Vytiper is commenced," Henry said.

They tiptoed down the hall of knights towards the sound of voices and music until they reached an archway that entered a ballroom.

Henry turned to Lang. "Good luck. Don't die before you get that watch off."

Lang smiled a little. "I'll try. Good luck to you too."

Henry nodded. "Let's go."

Persi hung back while Henry and Hattie turned into the ballroom and watched Lang and Morton disappear into the crowd. The room had a high ceiling with a giant chandelier in the middle. An orchestra on a stage played a plodding song in a minor key, and the people dressed in suits and gowns mingled with each other and ate from trays passed around by waiters. A few guards at the edge of the room watched the crowd intently.

"Do you see Jacoby anywhere?" Henry said.

Hattie scanned the room. "By the sweets table. He's alone, just looking around...

duck!" Henry ducked down into the crowd.

Hattie pretended to smooth a wrinkle out of her dress and whispered, "He looked over here, but I don't think he noticed you. I have an idea. Watch from here and be prepared to move."

She wove through the crowd toward the watchful Jacoby. Henry poked his head around a large woman draped with musty brown ruffles. He watched Jacoby greet Hattie with a nod and she poured herself a glass of pomegranate blood from the buffet table. In a swift movement, she lurched forward and sloshed the juice onto Jacoby's gloved hand and arm.

"Nice going, Hattie," Henry said to himself.

Jacoby's face changed from placid to a momentary irritation, and back to his usual downturned expression. Hattie apologized, and Jacoby nodded and excused himself. She rushed back and grabbed Henry's arm.

"He's going to the bathroom, quick."

They scurried across the ballroom floor, trailing Jacoby. Out of the corner of his eye, Henry spotted Lang and Morton crouched at the side of the room, but men in deep green suits moved and blocked his view. Jacoby left through the archway they had entered through and went into the bathroom. Henry spied a few pink hair strands sticking out from the side of the dining room entrance. They hesitated in front of the door.

"You should stay here," Henry said.

Hattie cocked her head. "Are you sure?"

"Yeah. I want to do this alone."

She nodded in understanding and Henry gave her one last look. He turned the knob to the bathroom and entered, the door closing behind him with a thud. There at the sink was Jacoby Dread and no one else. The two were alone.

Jacoby had removed his glove and Henry's eyes shot to his hand. His hunch had been right. Curled around Jacoby's pointer finger like a snake was the small hour hand from Henry's pocket watch. The last piece of the puzzle.

Jacoby turned his attention from his hand to the mirror and saw the boy standing in the reflection. Their eyes met and he calmly put his glove on. "Henry. I should have guessed."

"I thought it was interesting you only wore one glove."

"That's none of your business. Now leave before I kick you out."

"I don't really see that happening."

Jacoby placed the palms of his hands on the sink edge. "Ferdinand," he commanded. In a mere second, the butler walked through the bathroom door and stood behind Henry. "Take care of this problem, would you?"

Henry felt the cold grip of Ferdinand's hand on his wrist. Jacoby started for the door. "By the way, your suit is too big."

Ferdinand yanked Henry's shoulder to the side and Jacoby opened the door.

"Get him!" Henry shouted to his comrades.

He twisted out of Ferdinand's grasp and made a run towards Jacoby in the doorframe, Jacoby turned to face him. In a swirl of pink, purple and black, Hattie and Persi appeared from behind and locked themselves onto each arm. To Jacoby's shock, Henry reached forward and pinched the tip of the cloth glove. It slid off easily, once again revealing the hour hand within reach.

Jacoby came to his senses and flailed his arms, trying to shake the girls off. His face became cherry red and he gritted his teeth. Henry stuffed the glove into his suit pocket and stepped past the flinging trio out of the way of Ferdinand, who marched forward and gripped the two girls by the arm. With surprising strength, he tore them away and pinned them in place. Jacoby panted from his efforts.

"Persi, Hattie, keep Ferdinand busy," Henry said. "I'll take care of Jacoby."

"Get him, Bats," Persi said while biting Ferdinand's arm.

Hattie pulled against the butler's grip with all her might. "Go!"

Jacoby made a run for it toward the opposite direction of the ballroom. Henry followed close behind through the rows of knights to a side exit, his watch bumping against his chest with every step. The fog lay thick and heavy, its moisture coating his lungs and blurring his vision. His heart beat fast with only one thought: get the hour hand. He was so close.

Jacoby ran past his guards outside.

"Mr Dread?" one questioned, seeing Henry in pursuit.

"Don't leave your posts," he spat.

He ran straight to the end of Sable Avenue to the place where it had all began, the cemetery. He slowed down and passed through the gate to the tombstones and mausoleums. Henry followed, barely able to see the grave markers below him through the fog. It was silent except for their footsteps, which halted when Jacoby reached his own crypt. He opened the door and placed his hand on the empty marble casket. Henry stopped only a few feet away.

"You must have decoded the book to have gotten this far." Jacoby's dark eyes pierced through the mist.

"Hattie figured it out."

"I should have known. And you, Henry Bats, are brighter than I thought. Or maybe it was your friend."

Henry stepped closer. "Who was Zachary Dread?"

"My grandfather. He was the first Vytiper."

"And Ezekiel?"

"Zachary used his brother the first time to become a Vytiper to test the effects. Ezekiel went to the GrimMan for a reversal. He was successful up until the point you're at now."

"I'm going to finish it," Henry said.

The edges of Jacoby's mouth slowly pulled out and up, the first time Henry had seen him smile. "There's something you've forgotten, Henry."

He crossed his arms. "Yeah, what?"

Jacoby's fingertips on the tomb turned from a sickly green to a deep, endless black. "That I am no longer a human. I am a Vytiper."

The black spread to the rest of his body. The fog that surrounded the crypt seemed to buzz and electrify Henry's skin.

Jacoby's being separated into the shadow creature that had first woken Henry from his sleep. Only this time, the shadow had two tunnels for eyes and a gaping mouth filled with white, pointed teeth. Jacoby spoke, his voice a low, distorted growl.

"You can't escape."

A gust of wind blew through Henry's hair. He stumbled backwards but didn't run.

The smile grew wider. "I'm not afraid to end your life, Henry."

"And just how are you going to do that?"

Jacoby snapped his pointed mouth closed. "With these jaws."

"I'm not afraid of you."

"Why is that, Henry?"

"Because today isn't the day I'm supposed to die."

Jacoby's laughter vibrated through the fog. "It wasn't Ezekiel's day either, but Zachary was still able to dispose of him. The GrimMan loves to play with lives."

The shadow that was Jacoby grew larger and larger until

it was ten times its original size. He opened his mouth filled with flashing teeth and descended down upon Henry. Henry jumped out of the way, dirt flying from his shoes pushing into the ground. Blood pumping, he ran behind a crypt and crouched down. He controlled his breath and stayed as still as possible.

"I know you're here, Henry," said Jacoby's booming voice. "If you come out now, I'll make it as painless as possible."

He slowly peeked from around the crypt. There was Jacoby, silently floating around the graveyard, and growing larger. Henry knew he couldn't avoid being seen for long. He had to act. Counting to three in his head, he jumped up.

"Hey, over here."

Jacoby's eye holes swiveled around on the black mass to look at him. "Giving up?"

"I want to make a truce. I won't bother you anymore if you don't bother me."

"It's too late, Henry. You're a threat. Now stand still."

Henry backed up as Jacoby slithered towards him.

"Hattie won't be happy with you. She'll know. She'll go to the police."

"There'll be no evidence left. I'm going to swallow you whole."

Henry gulped. "I don't really think I would taste good."

Jacoby's smile stretched further and he hovered above the boy. He opened his mouth, ready to plunge down. Henry stared, paralyzed, into the gaping hole that was now descending upon him. He watched as the teeth surrounded his body and he stared into the black abyss beyond. It closed in around him.

Chapter 15

Langley Skullfield Reaches His Fate

All Henry could see was darkness. It wasn't the kind of darkness like the Grimworld skies, but a true, empty black. Above him and below him was an expanse of nothing. He walked forward, his feet making no sound. He felt weightless. He wondered if he was dead. But ahead he saw something, a dot of color. He ran, unable to hear his own breathing. Finally, he was able to make out a human figure, an older man sitting in a rocking chair. He wore a clean tan suit. Henry slowed as he got closer.

The man looked up, his face etched with lines, his dark eyes tired. "Hello," the man said.

"Hello," said Henry.

They looked at each other. The man was familiar to Henry. "Who are you?"

"I'm Ezekiel Dread."

Henry remembered the two portraits before Jacoby's office. "You're Ezekiel?"

"Do you have cotton in your ears?"

"No. I was just surprised."

He shifted in his chair. "Why is that? Have you heard of me?"

"Yes. Your brother's grandson, Jacoby, just swallowed me."

"Ah, an offspring of Zachary. I'm not surprised." His eyes floated down to Henry's neck. "I see you have a pocket watch."

"Yeah."

"I have one too." Ezekiel reached into his suit and pulled out a bronze pocket watch with an alligator in the center.

"My friend Lang and I found your note in the Vytiper book. We put the ingredients in the compartment, and I was trying to get the hour hand back when Jacoby swallowed me and I ended up here."

"Yes, I see that."

Henry looked around. "Where is here, exactly?"

"I'm not entirely sure, myself. I was at the same point as you, until my brother swallowed me."

"Am I dead? Are you even real?"

"Both are quite possible. There's a theory I've been working on. I think because it wasn't my time to die yet, by swallowing me, my brother messed everything up and put me in some kind of limbo."

"What's a limbo?"

"It means I'm to be stuck here forever."

Henry knitted his eyebrows together. "Oh."

"So you say you just need the hour hand?"

"Yes."

"You know, this Jacoby is quite the powerful Vytiper. I should know, I lived in my brother's stomach."

Henry shook his head. "I think I'm going crazy," he muttered. "So what do I need to do?"

"I'll tell you what, I've been here for a while now and I think I've figured a way out."

"Really? Then why haven't you left?"

"By the time I figured it out, Zachary had ended his life as a Vytiper and my way out went poof."

"Why did he do that?"

"You sure do ask a lot of questions. That's good. My guess is he kept getting short lifespans and threw a tantrum."

"So could you help me?"

"I don't see why not." Ezekiel got out of his rocking chair and cleared his throat. "You see, my theory is that since we've been swallowed, we're in some kind of stomach."

"Makes sense."

"So what does one do when they need to get something out of their stomach?"

"Puke?"

"Something to that effect. Have you ever gotten food poisoning?"

Henry thought back to a few months ago and clutched his stomach. "Yeah, my mom made some bad chicken."

"Very good. Now, the Vytiper is a Shadow entity. What would upset a shadow?"

Henry thought about it. "Light?"

"Excellent." Ezekiel reached inside his suit pocket and pulled out an orange matchbox. "Luckily I had these when my brother swallowed me. You can do the honors."

Henry took the box from his hand and pulled out a red-tipped match. He slid it across the side of the box and it lit into a small flame. The light glimmered on their faces.

"Now what?"

"Drop it."

"What about you?"

Ezekiel sat down and took the matchbox. His chair gently rocked back and forth. "I will remain here. Perhaps I can help another like yourself."

"You don't get bored?"

"Plenty to think about."

"Well, if I figure a way to get you out, I will."

Ezekiel nodded and Henry dropped the match. They watched it fall and disappear into the darkness below, followed by a few puffs of smoke. Within seconds the smoke grew into a cloud that billowed upwards. Henry felt a tug on his body, as though he were being pulled backwards. He could barely make out the man in the rocking chair.

Ezekiel's voice cut through the smoke. "What was your name?"

"Henry Bats," he said, the pull on his body becoming stronger.

"Bats? Tell Flemm to keep lettuce prices under control."

Henry went flying backwards, Ezekiel growing smaller until

he was out of sight. The stench of smoke dizzied his head and his eyes closed. The pull on his body ceased abruptly as he landed with a thud. Henry felt himself lying on something hard and cold. The fire smell was gone.

He squinted his eyes open to see a purple light above him. A street lamp. His head rolled to the right and he saw the Sable Avenue cemetery through its black iron fence. He rolled his head to the left and saw Jacoby across the street on the sidewalk. He was in his human form, doubled over and violently coughing. Henry's gaze locked on the hour hand that spiraled around Jacoby's finger. This was his chance to get it off.

He rolled his head up off the ground and heaved his body to a sitting position. Jacoby glanced up from his hacking and noticed Henry, awake. He stumbled forward towards the cemetery.

Henry struggled to his feet and took a moment to regain his balance on the ground. The thick fog blustered around in a frenzy, urging him on. Through the purple light of the lamps, he ran back into the cemetery after Jacoby, who was headed for his crypt.

Henry gritted his teeth. "Not again."

Jacoby lurched ahead through coughs, clutching his stomach. Small smoke plumes puffed from his mouth. Henry sprinted, closing the gap between the two until he was only a few feet away. He veered to the right where Jacoby's left hand clasped his side and stretched his arm out. Henry leapt forward and grabbed the pointer finger looped with the hour hand.

Jacoby turned his head to the boy, his eyes growing wide. He jerked his arm away, but the hour hand slid off into Henry's grasp. The Vytiper stopped in his tracks, mouth hanging open.

The hour hand uncurled in Henry's palm into a straight line. He stepped back from Jacoby and lifted the pocket watch. The face opened easily and he pushed the hand onto the center knob. It latched on.

Jacoby closed his mouth. He rushed forward and grabbed

Henry's shoulder, but it was too late. Henry pushed the hour hand back to 12 o'clock and shut the watch face. He looked into Jacoby's dark, glaring eyes only inches from his own. They flashed from anger to shock, growing wide with terror. The hand on Henry's shoulder deepened in color to black and separated into a shadow. The black continued to Jacoby's arm, up his neck, and spread across his face. His entire body dissolved into the mist, leaving only his eyes. Henry watched as the darkness clouded over his stunned gaze. The eyes rolled back and then lifted upwards and slowly faded into the dark sky of Grimworld. All that remained was empty air.

A click sounded in Henry's ears. The chain around his neck broke and he felt the weight leave him as the pocket watch fell to the ground. The fog cleared away, leaving a circular patch of visibility. He stared at the watch with the odd feeling that something which he had grown used to was gone. The gold metal gleamed in the purple light. The crow's eye seemed to stare at him.

Henry bent down and closed his fingers around it. With plodding steps, he walked back into the Sable Avenue graveyard and stepped inside Jacoby's open crypt. He set the watch on the marble casket.

"You were greedy and wanted to live forever. But really, I think you just wanted to have tea parties."

Henry went to leave but glanced over his shoulder. "Don't come back to haunt me."

He ran up the street to Dread Manor. At the gate, he rushed past the guards, who were in the middle of eating sweets from the Ball. He went through the front door to the people dancing without any idea of what happened to their host and circled the ballroom looking for Persi and Hattie.

A sweaty hand gripped his. "Henry!"

He whirled around to find Hattie, pale-faced and breathing hard.

"I've been looking all over for you! Come quick. It's Lang."

Henry felt his stomach drop as Hattie pulled him through the room. "Did you get the hour hand?" he asked.

"No, we almost had it but Greta started pelting us with truffles and Lang just collapsed. Persi's still going after her."

"What about Ferdinand?"

"He was a problem, but all of a sudden he disappeared. Like smoke."

They moved into the dining hall, where Lang lay next to Morton.

"I have to help Persi," Hattie said and sprinted out.

Lang's eyes were closed and his breath was stilted. Henry crouched down and lifted his pocket watch. "The minute hand is on the one. He's out of time."

"What does that mean?" Morton said.

"It means he's dying." Henry gripped Lang's shoulder and shook it. "Hey. Are you awake?"

The corner of Lang's mouth twitched and he mumbled something inaudible. Henry bent down to listen. "What's that?"

"Sorry," he said faintly.

Henry pulled back and reached for Lang's cold hand. He sat quietly with Morton and watched his chest rise and fall as his breath became shallow. A lump formed in Henry's throat and he kept swallowing hard.

Persi burst into the room with Hattie. "We've got it."

Henry jumped up. "You've got it?"

Hattie darted to her brother and placed Greta's hour hand in his palm. "Is there still time?" she said, dropping down to Lang's side.

Henry knelt down with her. "I don't know. Where's Greta?"

"We locked her in the bathroom," Persi said.

He opened the watch face and quickly attached the hand. "Hang on, Lang." All it took was one swivel and the time was 12 o'clock.

Lang inhaled sharply and his breathing stabilized. His eyelids fluttered, opening to see the four frightened faces of his friends hovering over him. Tears flowed down the side of his face.

"I thought I saw my brother," he said.

Henry touched his arm. "Your time almost ran out. But we got the hour hand from Greta." He lifted Lang's pocket watch and gently pulled. The silver chain was already broken and he held it up. "See?"

Lang blinked. "I'm alive?"

"You're alive."

"What about you?"

"All good," Henry said and thumped his chest where the watch had rested. "Can you stand?"

Hattie helped Lang to his feet and he walked a few steps on his own. "I'm alright."

"Glad you didn't die," Persi said. "That Greta was pretty spry, I had to dodge a few punches for you."

"Thanks, Persi."

Hattie looked at Henry. "Well, your plan didn't turn out too badly. I guess you're not as dumb as I thought."

"You know, Jacoby said the same thing. You two have a lot in common."

She slapped his arm. "We most certainly do not."

"Guys, we should probably leave," Morton said.

They made their way out of the dining hall and through the ballroom. The attendees stopped their dancing and chatting to stare, mostly at Persi.

"Pink hair? Goodness."

"Those suits!"

"Has anyone seen Jacoby?"

They emerged into the still, foggy night and took one last look at Dread Manor.

"What'll happen to the place?" Henry said.

Lang shrugged. "The guards will realize Jacoby is gone and

eventually, they'll leave. It'll probably be abandoned."

"But space is tight around here, so someone'll snatch it up," Morton said.

"I wonder who." Henry gazed at the cherub fountain. "Anyways, let's get out of here."

They headed down Sable Avenue, the fog jumping up here and there in plumes.

"Hey, where did you get the pink hair dye?" Hattie asked Persi.

"Oh, I just pick it up from a hairdresser. If you stop by the Shady Phantom sometime I'll give you a box."

"The Shady Phantom?" Morton said. "Isn't there some kind of secret room in there?"

The three continued ahead while Henry and Lang walked silently behind. When they arrived back at Frank's, Morton shook all of their hands. "Hattie, if you're up to it you can write a case file on the Vytiper."

"Sure thing."

"I can't wait to tell the Club we have an in at the Shady Phantom. Great work everyone, I'll be on my way."

"See you guys later, I'll get you that hair dye, Hattie," Persi said.

"You're next to get your watch off, Persi," Henry said. "Prepare to rub some feet."

She winked and departed with Morton through the fog.

"Lang, will you come over for dinner sometime?" Hattie said.

"I'd be happy too."

Henry waved her away. "You go on ahead. I'll catch up."

"Fine. See you soon, Lang. I'm so relieved you got your watch off."

The two boys were left in front of Frank's cartoon snake sign. Henry smiled. "We did it."

Lang smiled back. "Yeah. What happened with Jacoby?"

"Well, he led me to the cemetery and turned into the shadow

Vytiper form and...you know what? How about I tell you at RIP tomorrow?"

"Sounds good. Right now I want to see my dad."

Henry nodded and held out his hand. "I'll see you tomorrow, friend."

Lang took it. "See you tomorrow."

Henry continued home through the fog, a Gloom Ghast behind him. Lang's voice from down the street reached his ears. "Don't forget we have to go to the worm lady's house again!"

Henry looked up at the black sky of Grimworld and shuddered. "I hate worms."

About Avery Moray

Avery Moray is a storyteller specializing in middle grade and young adult fantasy. She lives in a land with tall mountains and wide plains with her two furry sidekicks and one non-furry accomplice. She likes sweets, cats, and Halloween, and loves creating things of all kinds, stories being one of them. You can visit her website below for more story content.

Follow Avery Moray
Twitter: @landofbooksam
Instagram: @landofbooksam
www.landofbooksam.com

A message from Avery Moray

I'm so delighted that you've read Grimworld, and I hope you feel that you've had adventures with new friends that will always be there if you need them. Please look forward to more stories from me in the future, new lands and characters await!

**OUR STREET
BOOKS**

JUVENILE FICTION, NON-FICTION, PARENTING

Our Street Books are for children of all ages, delivering a potent
mix of fantastic, rip-roaring adventure and fantasy stories to excite
the imagination; spiritual fiction to help the mind and the heart;
humorous stories to make the funny bone grow; historical tales to
evolve interest; and all manner of subjects that stretch
imagination, grab attention, inform, inspire and keep the pages
turning. Our subjects include Non-fiction and Fiction, Fantasy and
Science Fiction, Religious, Spiritual, Historical, Adventure, Social
Issues, Humour, Folk Tales and more.
If you have enjoyed this book, why not tell other readers by
posting a review on your preferred book site.

Recent bestsellers from Our Street Books are:

Relax Kids: Aladdin's Magic Carpet
Marneta Viegas
Let Snow White, the Wizard of Oz and other fairytale characters
show you and your child how to meditate and relax. Meditations
for young children aged 5 and up.
Paperback: 978-1-78279-869-9 Hardcover: 978-1-90381-666-0

Wonderful Earth
An interactive book for hours of fun learning
Mick Inkpen, Nick Butterworth
An interactive Creation story: Lift the flap, turn the wheel, look in
the mirror, and more.
Hardcover: 978-1-84694-314-0

Boring Bible: Super Son Series 1
Andy Robb
Find out about angels, sin and the Super Son of God.
Paperback: 978-1-84694-386-7

Jonah and the Last Great Dragon
Legend of the Heart Eaters
M.E. Holley
When legendary creatures invade our world, only dragon-fire can
destroy them; and Jonah alone can control the Great Dragon.
Paperback: 978-1-78099-541-0 ebook: 978-1-78099-542-7

Little Prayers Series: Classic Children's Prayers
Alan and Linda Parry
Traditional prayers told by your child's favourite creatures.
Hardcover: 978-1-84694-449-9

Magnificent Me, Magnificent You The Grand Canyon
Dawattie Basdeo, Angela Cutler
A treasure filled story of discovery with a range of inspiring fun exercises, activities, songs and games for children aged 6 to 11.
Paperback: 978-1-78279-819-4

Q is for Question
An ABC of Philosophy
Tiffany Poirier
An illustrated non-fiction philosophy book to help children aged 8 to 11 discover, debate and articulate thought-provoking, open-ended questions about existence, free will and happiness.
Hardcover: 978-1-84694-183-2

Relax Kids: How to be Happy
52 positive activities for children
Marneta Viegas
Fun activities to bring the family together.
Paperback: 978-1-78279-162-1

Rise of the Shadow Stealers
The Firebird Chronicles
Daniel Ingram-Brown
Memories are going missing. Can Fletcher and Scoop unearth their own lost history and save the Storyteller's treasure from the shadows?
Paperback: 978-1-78099-694-3 ebook: 978-1-78099-693-6

Readers of ebooks can buy or view any of these bestsellers by clicking on the live link in the title. Most titles are published in paperback and as an ebook. Paperbacks are available in traditional bookshops. Both print and ebook formats are available online.

Find more titles and sign up to our readers' newsletter at
http://www.johnhuntpublishing.com/children-and-young-adult
Follow us on Facebook at https://www.facebook.com/JHPChildren
and Twitter at https://twitter.com/JHPChildren